THE 3 INVESTIGATORS

CRIMEBUSTERS™ #2

Murder To Go

by
**MEGAN STINE &
H. WILLIAM STINE**

based on characters created by Robert Arthur

Borzoi Sprinters
ALFRED A. KNOPF · NEW YORK

DR. M. JERRY WEISS, Distinguished Service Professor of Communications at
Jersey City State College, is the educational consultant for Borzoi Sprinters.
A past chair of the International Reading Association President's Advisory
Committee on Intellectual Freedom, he travels frequently to give workshops
on the use of trade books in schools.

A BORZOI SPRINTER PUBLISHED BY ALFRED A. KNOPF, INC.
Copyright © 1989 by Random House, Inc.
All rights reserved under International and Pan-American Copyright
Conventions. Published in the United States by Alfred A. Knopf, Inc.,
New York, and simultaneously in Canada by Random House of Canada
Limited, Toronto. Distributed by Random House, Inc., New York.

CRIMEBUSTERS is a trademark of Random House, Inc.

Library of Congress Cataloging-in-Publication Data
Stine, Megan.
Murder to go / by Megan Stine & H. William Stine ;
based on characters created by Robert Arthur.
p.   cm.—(The 3 investigators. Crimebusters ; #2)
"A Borzoi sprinter."
Summary: The Three Investigators look into a rumor of poisoning
in a fast-food chain.
ISBN 0-394-89980-6 (pbk.)
[1. Mystery and detective stories. 2. Restaurants, lunch rooms, etc.—
Fiction.]   I. Stine, H. William.   II. Title.   III. Series: 3 investigators.
Crimebusters ; #2.
PZ7.S86035Mu 1989 [Fic]—dc19 88-14693

RL: 5.4

Also available in a library edition from Random House, Inc.—
ISBN 0-394-99980-0

Manufactured in the United States of America
10 9 8 7 6 5 4 3 2 1

1

Smashing Beauty

PETE CRENSHAW ZIPPED HIS CAR INTO THE OUTDOOR parking lot of Rocky Beach Memorial Hospital and hit the brakes. He revved the engine of the used '81 Scirocco a couple of times, loud and hard, then switched off the ignition. The windshield wipers stopped in the middle of their arc.

Pete liked to think he was just like his car—lean, mean, and prone to quick moves. At over six feet tall and built like a decathlon athlete, he wasn't far wrong.

"Wow. This is serious rain. And I mean *serious*," Pete said to his friend Jupiter Jones, who was sitting next to him.

Jupiter Jones was neither lean nor mean. He preferred to describe himself as "well padded" or "husky." He never seemed to run out of substitutes for "overweight." Most people would have laughed at Jupe's attempts to disguise the truth. But Pete kept the teasing to a minimum. After all, seventeen-year-old Jupiter was Pete's best friend. And Jupe was also the founder of The Three Investigators. Along with Bob Andrews, they were Rocky Beach, California's most famous detectives.

The two of them sat in the car and watched the storm. It was more than the typical summer downpour. Rain pounded the windshield. Then, just when Pete and Jupe were least expecting it, lightning flashed and crashed.

"Come on. It's never going to let up," Pete said, brushing his reddish-brown hair out of his eyes. "And visiting hours are almost over. Kelly's waiting for me."

"You can't let girls boss you around," Jupe said, unbuckling his seat belt reluctantly.

"I hate to tell you this," Pete said to Jupe, "but girls are the one subject you're not an expert on."

"True," Jupe admitted. "However, as you well know, that won't stop me from giving you advice."

Pete laughed.

Then the two friends pulled up the hoods of their Windbreakers and made a dash through the rain for the hospital entrance.

Inside the hospital lobby they shook out their wet jackets and hurried to room 2113.

When they got there, Kelly Madigan was lying in her hospital bed, talking on the phone and twirling a curl of her long brown hair with her fingers. The TV was on, playing music videos with the sound off. She didn't look like someone who had just had her appendix taken out three days ago.

Kelly was a pretty, energetic cheerleader at Rocky

Beach High School, the same school Pete, Jupe, and Bob attended. One day six months ago she suddenly decided that Pete Crenshaw ought to be going steady and he ought to be going steady with her. Pete didn't put up much of a fight.

"Gotta hang up, Sue," Kelly said, giving Pete and Jupe a small wave. "Time for my Friday night date. My own personal hunk just walked in with a friend." Then Kelly laughed. "Is the friend a hunk too?" Kelly said, repeating what Sue had just asked her. She looked Jupe up and down with her large green eyes.

Jupe tried to stare back at her but then he got nervous and looked away.

"Depends, Sue," Kelly said. "Do you think Frosty the Snowman's a hunk?" she added with a teasing but sweet laugh.

Jupe crossed his arms and sat down grumpily on one of the uncomfortable wooden chairs that were standard in hospital rooms.

Suddenly Kelly held out the phone—to Jupe! "Sue wants to talk to you," she said, smiling.

Jupe swallowed hard and tried to look as though he didn't know the meaning of the word "panic." Talking to suspects in a mystery was no problem. Talking to girls—that was Bob Andrews' department.

"Go on, Jupe," Pete teased. He was sitting on the bed next to Kelly.

Jupe slowly stood up and took the phone.

"Hello," he said formally, "this is Jupiter Jones speaking." Jupe paused.

"Hi," said a girl's voice with a nervous giggle. "I'm Sue. How's it going?"

"How is what going?" Jupe asked. His logical mind required logical questions before he could give a logical answer.

"Oh, I don't know, you know," said Sue.

Jupe cleared his throat and squinted one eye at Kelly. He wished he didn't have an audience for this phone call. Pete and Kelly were holding hands and grinning at him.

"Don't you want to know if I'm cute or something?" Sue asked on the other end of the line.

Just then a nurse with bright copper-red hair stuck her head in the door. "Visiting hours are over. You'll have to leave now," she said.

Jupe sighed with relief and handed the phone back to Kelly. "I'll call you later," Kelly told Sue, hanging up quickly. Then she winked at Jupe. "Jupiter Jones, ladies' man, strikes again," she said.

Suddenly the door banged open. A doctor, two orderlies, and two nurses pushed a gurney into the room at top speed. Jupe had to jump out of the way.

They had a patient on the gurney, a young woman with dark curly hair. Her pretty face was pale, bruised, and bandaged. She was unconscious.

"New roommate for you, Kelly," said the doctor, a young intern with a short ponytail and a calm smile. He helped lift the new patient onto the second bed in Kelly's green hospital room.

"Is she hurt badly?" Kelly asked.

"Her wounds appear superficial," Jupe said. His eyes never missed anything. "My guess is she's just recovering from a concussion and mild shock."

"Hey—great diagnosis," the doctor said, looking over at Jupe with a surprised smile.

The hospital team gently settled the young woman into the bed and then hooked up her i.v., which started the medication dripping. When they were certain she was secure, the nurses and orderlies backed away and the doctor wrote notes on her chart.

"What happened to her?" Kelly asked the doctor in a concerned voice.

"Car smash-up on Countyline Drive. She went right off the road. We always get a couple on a rotten night like this," he said, moving toward the door to leave. "She's a celebrity's kid, although it's hard to tell with all the bumps and bruises. She's—"

But before the doctor could finish his sentence, the nurse with the copper-red hair opened the door again. "I said it once. I'll say it again," she barked at Jupe and Pete. "Hospital visiting hours are over. This means you must leave immediately. The only exception is if you are very sick, in which case please see the admissions nurse."

"We get the message," Pete said.

"Good," said the nurse with a pinched smile. "I guess I won't have to call out the guard dogs tonight."

As she turned and left the room, Pete leaned down and gave Kelly a quick kiss. "See you tomorrow, babe. I'm staying at Jupe's tonight."

Jupe, however, was looking at the new patient's chart.

"Hey—what are you doing?" Pete asked.

"Just satisfying my curiosity," Jupe answered. "The doctor left before telling us who she is. Who's Juliet Coop?"

Pete looked at Jupe and shrugged. The name didn't set off any bells. So they said good-bye to Kelly and left.

But a minute later both Pete and Jupe knew exactly who Juliet Coop was, because as they headed toward the elevator a huge man came rushing out of it and went straight to the nurses' station. He leaned over the desk so that his worried face was close to the nurse with the copper-colored hair. "Where's my daughter?" he asked. "Where is she?"

"That's Big Barney Coop!" Jupe said, recognizing the man instantly.

"Right. The Chicken King!" Pete exclaimed.

It had to be. He was wearing the familiar red, white, and blue jogging suit, just like the one he wore on TV. And everyone in Southern California knew Big Barney Coop's face. You couldn't flip the TV channels without seeing him in a commercial for Chicken Coop fast-food restaurants.

"Juliet Coop—Barney Coop," said Jupe. "She must be the Chicken King's daughter."

"Room 2113, Mr. Coop," said the nurse.

"Is that a lucky room?" asked Big Barney. "I want

my daughter in a lucky room. Where is it? Which way? Which room?"

Jupiter felt sorry seeing Big Barney so upset and disoriented. He walked over to the nurse's desk. "Mr. Coop, it's that room," Jupe said, pointing.

Big Barney Coop, who was practically a foot taller than Jupe, looked down. "You sure?" he asked.

"My friend and I were visiting the patient who's sharing your daughter's room," Jupe said. "As a matter of fact, Juliet is sleeping now."

That seemed to be enough reassurance to make the Chicken King relax a little. "Here are a couple of freebies," he said, handing Jupe two coupons from his sweatshirt pocket. "I like you, guy. Plump but tender. I'll bet you'd look great dipped in my secret golden batter. Thanks, guy."

Jupe smiled and watched Big Barney walk into the hospital room. Then he tore up the coupons.

"Hey!" Pete said, grabbing for the coupons, but too late. "Why'd you do that, Jupe?"

"My diet," Jupe said unhappily. "No fried foods allowed, remember?"

"Yeah, I remember," Pete said. "And you have to eat a piece of melon with every meal. Weird. But just because *you're* dieting doesn't mean *I* am. I *love* the Chicken Coop's fried chicken."

"Don't even talk about it," Jupe moaned. "I love it too. I can smell that crispy crust and juicy tender white meat right now."

They dashed out into the rain-soaked parking lot and Pete drove them back toward Jupe's house. Jupe lived with his Aunt Mathilda and Uncle Titus Jones, who owned a junkyard across the street. When Jupe, Pete, and Bob were kids, they hung around the junkyard together, especially when they were on a case. The Three Investigators even had their secret headquarters there, in a trailer that was hidden by junk. But now that they were seventeen years old, the trailer was no longer hidden, and they mostly hung around in Jupe's electronics workshop, which was right next door.

"Too bad we couldn't have heard the details of Juliet Coop's car crash," Jupe said. Then he noticed Pete looking at him out of the corner of his eye. "I know, I know. There's no sign of anything mysterious about it. I just have this feeling. Call it a premonition."

Finally Pete pulled into the junkyard and they splashed through the mud into Jupe's workshop. Inside were desks and countertops filled with high-tech electronic gadgets and parts, catalogs of modern surveillance equipment, tools, high school notebooks, empty pizza boxes, music tapes, and a couple of chairs. There was also an answering machine, and as always Jupe checked it first thing.

"Hi, guys," said a familiar voice on the message tape. It was Bob Andrews, the third Investigator. "Sorry I didn't make it over to the hospital tonight to see Kelly. I had to check out a new band for the agency because the boss is out of town. Then Jennifer called to remind me that we had a date, which came as a shock to me and an even bigger shock to Amy, who I was supposed to meet for a clambake on the beach. Guess those clams got rained out. Anyway, Jupe, maybe you can work out a data base computer program for me, to prevent accidents like this from happening. Think about it. Talk to you guys tomorrow."

"Bob works too hard at that talent agency." Jupe scowled as he turned off the answering machine.

"I know," Pete said with a smile. "All that work cuts into his dating time."

Jupe started tinkering with a small device that was supposed to read electronic lock combinations, and Pete busied himself at another table, cleaning out the sprayer of a new fuel injector for his car. They talked until it got very late.

They talked about Jupe's wish for a car, about not seeing Bob too much anymore because of his job, and about running into Big Barney Coop. And Jupe talked about Juliet Coop's accident. It drove him crazy not to know the details about something.

Suddenly the telephone rang, startling both Pete and Jupe. They looked at the clock. Nearly midnight. Pretty late for calls, even on a Friday night.

Jupe sat down in an old swivel chair. It had a Niagara Falls 1982 souvenir pillow for its cushion. "The Three Investigators," he said in an I-mean-business voice.

"Jupe, it's Kelly. Put me on the speaker phone, okay? I've got to talk to both of you."

"It's Kelly," Jupe said as he switched on the speaker phone.

Pete looked as surprised as Jupe. "What's going on, Kel?" Pete asked.

"Something weird," Kelly said. "Juliet Coop has been moaning and talking in her sleep."

Jupe got that feeling again. But he didn't want to jump to conclusions. "Bad dreams aren't uncommon after an accident like hers," Jupe said.

"Okay, okay," Kelly said impatiently. "But it's *what* she's dreaming about that freaks me. She keeps saying, 'Millions of people will die.'"

The words gave Jupe and Pete a chill.

"And that's not all," Kelly continued. "She keeps saying, 'He's poisoning the chicken. It's wrong. It's wrong.' And she sounds like she means it. I mean, it doesn't sound like a dream."

Pete let out a low whistle. "Heavy duty."

"I *told* you I had a feeling!" Jupe said.

"Yeah," said Pete. "But who knew it meant the Chicken King was poisoning my favorite food!"

2

After-hours Visitors

"**H**ELLO?" KELLY MADIGAN'S PUZZLED VOICE CAME out of the speaker phone in Jupe's workshop. "Are you guys still there?"

They were there, but their tongues were in shock. How many times had they eaten at a Chicken Coop restaurant in their lives? Hundreds? Thousands? Probably more for Jupe. How many times had they seen Big Barney Coop's friendly face on TV and heard his crazy but sincere voice telling them, "I've built my reputation selling legs and not pulling yours."

"Big Barney Coop . . . poisoning his food . . . ?" Pete said, shaking his head. His voice trailed off and his face got serious. "I can't believe it."

"And there's no reason why we should," Jupe said, having given the matter some thought. "As Aunt Mathilda frequently reminds me, the trouble with jumping to conclusions is you don't know what you're going to land in."

"What's that mean?" Pete said.

"It means," said Jupe, "we can't accuse Big Barney

Coop of *anything*. For one thing, there's no reason to think that Big Barney is the person Juliet was talking about in her sleep. It could be anyone who's poisoning the chicken. And for all we know, Juliet Coop is having a bad reaction to her medication or to the shock of her accident, or maybe she's just having bad dreams."

"Hey, guys," Kelly said, talking into her hospital phone. "I'd love to put Juliet on the line so you could talk to her personally, but the phone cord's not long enough to reach her in dreamland. Oh, listen . . . did you hear that?"

Pete shook his head. Jupe answered out loud, since Kelly couldn't see through the telephone. "No. What?" Jupe asked.

"She said it again," Kelly reported. "She said, 'No—people will die. Don't do it!' "

"Okay," Jupe said to Kelly. "We'll be there at eleven A.M. tomorrow to talk to Juliet. That's when visiting hours start. I'm certain she can tell us whether this was just a bad dream or not."

"Fine," Kelly said. "But I'm telling you there's a mystery here."

"See you in the morning, babe," Pete said, and hung up the phone.

Nobody got much sleep that night. For one thing, Jupe stayed up trying to figure out who would want to poison millions of people, and why. Was it Big Barney? Or was Juliet Coop mixed up with some kind of crazy political terrorist group? Or was there someone else who would want to poison the Chicken Coop's prime fillets?

Then at two in the morning Jupe called Bob Andrews to fill him in and to make sure he'd be at the hospital early too.

After the phone call, Bob had trouble falling back to sleep because he knew that when Jupe got into one of his agitated moods, he called frequently.

Kelly didn't sleep, either. She stayed awake in her hospital bed most of the night, waiting for Juliet Coop to say something more. Every time Juliet moaned in her bed, Kelly would ask her softly, "Who, Juliet? Who's poisoning the chicken?" But Juliet didn't answer.

Pete slept like a rock.

The next day bright sunlight filled Kelly's hospital room when Pete and Jupe arrived.

The first thing Jupe noticed—besides the fact that Kelly looked very tired, and that the number of vases of flowers in the room had quadrupled during the night, and that a large stuffed chicken wearing a golden crown now occupied the guest chair by Juliet's bed—was that the curtains had been drawn around Juliet Coop, sealing her off.

"Who's in there?" Jupe asked, pointing to the curtained area. He wanted to talk to Juliet right away and settle this mystery.

"Shhh." Kelly hushed Jupe and then spoke in a whisper. "No one's in there except Juliet. I think she's asleep."

Just then Bob Andrews walked in.

"Sorry I'm late guys. Car trouble," the tall, lanky teen said, taking off the cotton sweater that was tied around his neck.

Bob had always been a thin kid with glasses who was good at school but usually got lost in the background. Maybe it was because he worked for so many years in the dark, hidden stacks of the town library.

But all of that was changed now. Contact lenses, brighter clothes, a job with Sax Sendler's talent agency, a car of his own, karate lessons, and a lot of self-confidence had transformed The Three Investigators' researcher into one of the most popular guys at Rocky Beach High School.

"Where's our case? Or did the Chicken Princess fly the coop?" Bob asked.

"The case is behind the curtains," Pete said, motioning with a jerk of his head. "She's asleep. We can't talk to her."

"I'm sure that Jupe would be the first to point out that logically we *could* talk to her all we wanted," Bob said with a smile. "She just won't answer."

"At least she's quiet now," Kelly said softly. "You should have heard her moaning all night. And she had some interesting visitors."

"In the middle of the night?" Jupe said, surprised. "How'd they get past the nurse with the red hair and hot temper?"

Kelly shrugged. "Very mysterious, isn't it?"

"Who were they?" Jupe asked skeptically.

"Well, Big Barney was in here every hour. He even gave me a couple of free coupons," Kelly said.

"Who else?" asked Jupe.

"A good-looking guy named Sean Fellows," Kelly said.

"How do you know his name?" Pete asked, suddenly frowning.

"Because I asked him—and don't be so jealous," Kelly said. "He's Juliet's ex-boyfriend. He came at about four A.M. and just sat there watching her. Then early this morning there was another visitor, Maria Gonzales. She said she was Juliet's college roommate."

"We can forget about her," Jupe said.

"Why?" Bob asked.

"Because Juliet said, 'He's poisoning the chicken,' " Jupe explained. "And I'm not too worried about this Sean Fellows, either. An ex-boyfriend doesn't sound like someone who would kill millions."

"Not even for revenge?" Pete asked.

Jupe gave a "maybe" shrug.

"But you haven't heard about mystery guest number four," Kelly said, lowering her voice even more.

The four teenagers looked toward the closed curtains around Juliet's bed to be sure she wasn't waking up. Then Kelly continued her story. "The fourth person I call Mr. Sweetness," she said. "He was like a brick wall with a bad temper. He was big, in his thirties, wearing an army camouflage jacket. As soon as he saw me, he put the collar up to hide his face. Maybe 'cause he was so ugly!"

"Why didn't you ask *his* name?" said Pete grumpily.

"Hey—I *did*, and he told me to mind my own business. And he meant it," Kelly said. "Then he drew the curtains around Juliet's bed so I couldn't see anything."

"But what did you *hear*?" asked Jupe.

"Well," Kelly said, "I heard him go through her closet and after that, every drawer on her side of the room."

"Slowly or quickly?" Jupe asked.

"Quickly," Kelly answered with a decisive nod.

Jupe smiled. "From that I'd have to conclude that he wasn't just browsing. He knew exactly what he was looking for."

"But he didn't find it. He left empty-handed," Kelly added.

"Unfortunately, there's no way to get any more answers until Juliet wakes up," Jupe said, starting to pace the floor.

"And she'd better wake up during visiting hours or the dragon lady will kick us out again," Pete said.

Bob peeked around the corner of Juliet's curtains. "She doesn't look too bad," he said. "The newspaper this morning said she was lucky to be alive. She totaled her car in the crash." Bob turned back to his friends. "Have you been to the scene of the accident yet?"

Jupe shook his head and kept pacing back and forth. Just then the nurse with red hair came into the room carrying a large bouquet of flowers.

She looked at Kelly and then at each of the guys in the room. "Three boys?" she said, shaking her head at Kelly. "Don't you think you should let someone else have one?" She set the flowers down by Juliet's bed and then walked to the door. "I'll be back," she said, almost like a warning.

"What for?" Pete muttered when she was gone.

"Well, this is interesting," Bob said, examining the flowers the nurse had left. "These are from Michael Argenti."

"Why is that interesting?" asked Pete.

"Because he's the competition," Bob said. "He owns the Roast Roost restaurants."

"How do you know all this stuff? I mean, between you and Jupe, it's disgusting," Pete said.

Bob laughed. "No, it's just that one of the bands we handle at the agency just played at the grand opening of a new Roast Roost franchise. And Michael Argenti was supposed to be there, but he kept us waiting four hours in the hot sun until he showed up."

"Can you explain why Argenti would send flowers to the daughter of his rival?" asked Jupe.

"Sax does things like that sometimes," said Bob. "It's a business practice. Doesn't mean you actually like the guy. I heard Argenti and Big Barney can't stand each other. Every time Michael Argenti makes a wish on a wishbone, he wishes Big Barney would drop dead. And it's the same for Big Barney."

"Well, now at least we've got some suspects," Pete said, pounding his fist into his hand.

"Yeah, but do we have a crime?" Jupe asked.

At that moment Big Barney Coop opened the door. He froze for a second, obviously surprised at seeing a roomful of people.

Jupe studied Big Barney's full, round face. What was that deep in his eyes? Was it the look of a father worried for his daughter? Or was it the look of a maniac who didn't want his daughter to find out about his plot to poison the world?

Without walking into the room, Big Barney said, "How about giving me time alone with my daughter?"

Jupe, Pete, and Bob reluctantly moved out into the hallway. Jupe glanced around and then walked toward the nurses' station in the center of the hall. There was only one nurse behind the desk, the woman with the copper-red hair. Her nametag said ELIZABETH LAZAR, R.N.

"Could you tell me who was the nurse on duty last night?" Jupe asked.

"Funny you should ask," Nurse Lazar answered. "Not that it's any of your business, but it was *me*— that's who. One of the other nurses ran off and got married and I've been pulling triple shifts. Twenty-four hours straight."

Jupe smiled excitedly. "Great. Then perhaps you could tell me about Juliet Coop's three visitors," he said. "Besides her father."

Nurse Lazar frowned and shook her head. "No way. Patient info is strictly for the family."

The conversation was closed. Jupe could see it in

her eyes. She was tired, she was grumpy, she was a lot of things, but talkative wasn't one of them. Jupe sighed and looked away.

"It's really important," Bob said, running his hand through his blond hair.

She turned her stare on Bob, who smiled back.

Then he said in his most friendly voice, "Triple shifts, huh? What a bummer. How about if we personally sing you three choruses of the Beatles song of your choice—and, trust me on this, you haven't heard 'Sergeant Pepper' until you've heard us."

"Spare me the charm. I've had a long day," Nurse Lazar said. But her face actually thawed and she almost smiled. "Okay, look. There weren't three visitors last night. Only two—a young man and a young woman."

"What about the guy in the army jacket?" Jupe asked.

Elizabeth Lazar's eyebrows shot up in surprise. "I told him he couldn't go in," she said. "What a nerve! That guy gave me the creeps."

"Why?" Bob asked.

"He kept asking me questions," she said. "And he was asking some doozies."

"For example?" asked Jupe.

" 'Is she going to make it?'—he said it just like that. And 'Where is her personal property?' Questions like that. He didn't exactly look like a friend of the family, either."

"Did you get a good look at him?" Bob asked.

Nurse Lazar shook her head. "I'm not a face person," she said. "I remember his jacket and his questions. I could remember his temperature if I took it. Not his face."

"Thanks," Bob said.

As the Three Investigators turned away, Jupe said, "This Mr. Sweetness sounds suspicious to me. But maybe Juliet knows who he is. Let's go back in the room and see if she's awake."

"Hey, guys," said Nurse Lazar, shaking her head. "Juliet Coop was shaken up pretty badly, and her body needs to sleep it off. So she won't be awake for a while."

With that piece of news, the Three Investigators decided to take another approach. Jupe and Bob would do exactly what they'd done on a million other cases in the past. They'd go to Rocky Beach's police station to talk with their longtime ally, Chief Reynolds. Pete, on the other hand, would do exactly what Kelly told him to do—stay at the hospital and keep her company.

Bob jumped behind the wheel of his red VW bug, and Jupe squeezed into the passenger side.

In a little while, the two of them were sitting across from Chief Reynolds, watching him dig into his lunch—a box of Chicken Coop fried chicken.

"You guys want a piece?" the chief offered.

"Thanks," Bob said, dipping into the cardboard box, which pictured a chicken wearing a crown.

Jupe gripped his chair with both hands and tried to say "no, thanks" as calmly as he could.

"So what are The Three Investigators up to now?" asked the chief as he gnawed happily on a leg.

"We wanted to know the circumstances of Juliet Coop's accident," Jupe said.

"No mystery there," said the police chief through a mouthful of chicken. "She lost control of her car on a hill in the rain and crashed. Beginning, middle, and end."

"Isn't there anything strange about the case?" Jupe asked.

"A couple of questions to be cleared up, but there always are," said the chief. "For one thing, the accident was reported anonymously. We'd like to track down the citizen who called us. Maybe it was a witness. But why didn't he give his name? Also, there were two sets of tire skid marks—one from Juliet's car, going straight off the road, and another set beside hers. They ended farther down the hill from where she crashed."

Jupe tried to imagine it. He saw two cars coming down the hill. Juliet's car was in front and someone else—who?—was behind her. Jupe pinched his lower lip and visualized different scenarios.

"Chief Reynolds," Jupe said slowly. "Have you considered the possibility that Juliet Coop was being chased?"

3

Juliet's Romeo

"JULIET COOP BEING CHASED?" SAID CHIEF REYNOLDS, putting down his plastic cup of coleslaw and staring at the young detective. "What's your thinking, Jupe? Because that's a skinny limb you're standing on."

"It's an entirely logical possibility," Jupe said, leaning back in his chair. "If you were driving down a hill in the rain and the car in front of you skidded off the shoulder, what would you do?"

Bob spoke up first. "If I hit the brakes hard, I'd probably skid and stop down the road."

"Exactly where we found the second pair of tire tracks," Chief Reynolds added.

"But what would you do next?" Jupe asked.

"I'd probably back up the hill on the shoulder," Bob said. "That way I wouldn't have to run so far in the rain, and I could get to the other car faster."

"Exactly," Jupiter said with a triumphant smile. "Did the second car back up to try to help Juliet? Or even to find out if she was alive?"

"Not according to the evidence," the chief admitted. "We didn't find any fresh tire tracks or footprints in the soft, muddy shoulder. I'd have to say the second car just sat there."

"Who would just sit in a car and not help a driver who went off the road?" Jupe asked, and then answered himself. "Perhaps it was someone who was chasing Juliet Coop—and didn't care if she *died* in that crash!"

"It's a good theory," said Chief Reynolds. "You have any evidence?"

"We're working on it," Jupe said, standing up to leave. "Come on, Bob."

Chief Reynolds called to them before they got to the door. "Don't work too hard," he said. "As soon as the Chicken King's daughter wakes up, we'll get the whole story."

It was true, Jupe realized. When Juliet woke up, she *could* tell them whether someone had been following her before the crash. Maybe the other car had even tried to force her off the road. And maybe the driver of the other car was the person who was going to poison the chicken!

Juliet had all the answers in her sleepy head, and the Three Investigators would just have to wait.

But the real question was, would Juliet tell the truth when she woke up? If her father was somehow involved in this poison chicken thing, would she lie to protect him?

As Jupe and Bob left police headquarters and got into Bob's car, Jupe's stomach growled audibly.

"You know, Jupe, it's great that you're sticking to your diet and eveything. But no fried foods and then eating melon at every meal? It's weird," Bob said.

"Easy for you to say. Do you have a single shirt with a tag that says Extra-Large?"

Bob recognized Jupe's "discussion closed" tone of voice. "Okay. Sorry," he said. "So what's your plan now?"

"It's obvious that we have only one route to follow," Jupe answered. "Who was driving the car that was following Juliet Coop? It could have been one of the three people who visited her in the hospital last night."

"You mean Sean Fellows, Maria Gonzales, and that guy Kelly calls Mr. Sweetness," said Bob.

"Yes. And we've got to find out more about Michael Argenti, too—Big Barney's rival," Jupe said. "I can handle that with the computer back in Headquarters. I'll tap into DataServe and search their business files for everything about Michael Argenti and Roast Roost. *The Wall Street Journal* is in their data base. It should be informative. While I'm doing that, I want you to find out where Sean Fellows was last night before he came to the hospital."

"Can't handle it," Bob said apologetically. "Sax needs me at the agency."

"All right, then call Pete at the hospital and get him to take up the slack."

"No problem. But what about Maria and Mr. Sweetness?"

"I'm not too worried about Maria," said Jupe. "She doesn't seem to have any motive whatsoever. But I'll call her and check her out. As for Mr. Sweetness, we'll just have to wait until we cross paths."

Just then Jupe's stomach growled again. So Bob drove him to a supermarket to pick up another ten pounds' worth of watermelon. Then he dropped Jupe off at The Jones Salvage Yard and drove on to work. From there Bob called Pete at the hospital and gave him the assignment: Check out Juliet's ex-boyfriend, Sean Fellows.

But by the time Pete pulled himself away from Kelly, it was dark—too dark to find Sean's address. So it wasn't until Sunday that Pete pulled up in front of 23 Laurel Street, where Sean lived.

Sean Fellows' house was in a quiet and pretty neighborhood of Melton, a few miles north of Rocky Beach. The street was lined with small white wooden houses that had wide front porches and small front yards.

There was an old Bonneville convertible parked in front of Sean Fellows' house. And sitting on the porch railing was a guy with a blond flattop. He wore faded blue jeans and a white T-shirt with a leather vest. He jumped to his feet the moment Pete stepped into his yard.

"Come on!" he shouted, motioning with one hand to Pete and holding the other behind his back. "Make my day!" As soon as Pete was close to the porch, the hidden hand came out—holding a motorcycle chain!

What was going on? Pete's mind raced as his heart started thumping. Suddenly, for no reason, some maniac was coming at him with a vengeance. The guy had the motorcycle chain wrapped a couple of times around his hand, but its long tail swung freely. Pete froze in his tracks. Should he try some of his new karate moves? Or back off?

"Just you and me this time," the guy called to Pete. "That's what you want, isn't it?" His arm swung, and the tail of the vicious chain clattered and ripped into the wooden porch railing.

Forget the karate, thought Pete. He started to back away.

"I'm going to tear you open!" the guy yelled, jumping off the porch. He wasn't very big. In fact, he was much shorter and smaller built than Pete. But his voice was full of anger and he was swinging the chain wildly.

"You're making a big mistake," Pete said as he backed farther away. The guy kept coming, his black leather boots eating up the ground between them. His shoulders hulked like a gorilla's.

"I don't know what you think, but I'm looking for Sean Fellows," Pete said desperately. "I'm a friend of Juliet Coop's."

The black boots stopped walking, the chain stopped swinging.

"For real?" asked the guy.

Pete nodded his head but kept his fist clenched, ready to fight.

"Oh, well, uh, sorry," the guy said, letting out his breath. His whole body seemed to relax. "I'm Sean Fellows. I've been having some trouble here with a bunch of punk vandals. One of them just called and threatened to steal my car."

Sean motioned to the old beat-up Bonneville parked on the street. Pete stared at it.

"Maybe you should let him have it," Pete finally said with a laugh. "I mean, the tires are flat, it's leaking oil all over the ground . . ."

"Yeah, and besides that, the battery's been dead for two weeks!" Sean said, laughing too. "But I'm just sick of taking it from punks, you know what I mean?" Then he noticed his porch railing. "Don't tell me I destroyed my porch for nothing. Hey—how do you know Juliet?"

"Well, I don't really," Pete admitted. "She's in the hospital bed next to my girlfriend, Kelly."

"Oh, yeah," Sean said as he led Pete into his house. Now that he wasn't swinging a chain, Sean just seemed like a nice, average college student whose apartment had more posters than furniture.

"So why were you at the hospital so late Friday night?" Pete asked.

"Maria—Juliet's roommate in college—called me and said Juliet had been in an accident," Sean said.

"We only broke up a few months ago, Julie and I. I guess I'm not over her yet. I had to see if she was okay. Is she? Did she wake up yet?"

"Still out," Pete said. "At least, she's sleeping most of the time. The doctors say she needs a lot of rest."

Sean eyed Pete sideways for a moment. "Tell me something," Sean said, suddenly realizing that Pete was a complete stranger. "If you don't even know Juliet, what are you doing here, asking questions?"

"Kelly, my girlfriend, thinks something strange is going on," Pete said. "So I'm just checking it out. What do you know about Big Barney?"

"Big Barney? We'd still be going together if it weren't for him."

"What's that mean?" Pete asked.

"Her dad and I argued all the time," Sean said. "I'm a vegetarian, you know. No meat, no fish, no chicken. I don't believe in going around killing animals—or in anybody getting rich from slaughtering them. Barney hated my guts and he wasn't quiet about it. After a while, Juliet and I started fighting about it too. So when she said she was going to work for her father after graduation, that was about it."

"One last question and then I'll get outta here," Pete said. "How'd you get into the hospital at four A.M.?"

"I lied to the nurse, told her Julie and I were engaged," Sean admitted. "Wishful thinking, I guess."

Later that afternoon in The Jones Salvage Yard, Pete retold Sean Fellows' story to Jupe and Bob. As he

talked, Pete stooped down into the engine in the back
of Bob's VW. The fan belt was ancient and needed
replacing. Pete was putting a new one on. Once the
belt was positioned on the pulleys, he checked the
tension by pressing on it with his thumb.

"It's got to give about a half inch," Pete explained.
"And we'll have to tighten it up again after two hundred miles, 'cause these suckers stretch."

Ignoring the fan belt, Jupe said, "To me, the most
interesting thing in Pete's account is that Sean Fellows
owns a car."

"Jupe," Bob said, "sometimes I don't get you. Pete
just told us a tragic story of love destroyed because
of . . . of . . . dietary differences! And you shoot back
with an off-the-wall comment like that."

"Remember our goal," Jupe said. "We are pursuing
a suspect who was chasing Juliet Coop in a car."

"Forget Sean's car," Pete said. "The tires are flat
and the battery has been dead for two weeks."

"How do you know?" Jupe demanded.

"I checked with the neighbors," Pete answered.
"They confirmed his story."

"Ah." Jupe sighed. "Proof—there's no substitute for
it. Still, he sounds like a fairly violent person, with
that chain."

Pete shrugged as he turned the ignition on to test
the engine throttle. It hummed for a minute and then
made a sound something like *huppa-huppa-gak*.

"What does it mean when it makes that sound,
Pete?" Bob asked.

"It's car talk for 'Trade me—I'm falling apart,' " Pete said, laughing.

Bob was used to being teased about his antique car, and he laughed too. "Could you be a little more specific?" he asked.

"All I can say is there's more wrong than I have time to fix right now. I'll have to work on it. Maybe next week. Now, what about Maria Gonzales and Michael Argenti?" Pete asked Jupe.

Jupe smiled. "I called Maria and she's got an unbreakable alibi for the time of the accident—she was trapped in an elevator with six other people. But Michael Argenti is another story. As you know, he's Big Barney's main rival. But according to *The Wall Street Journal*, Argenti recently tried to buy out Big Barney and take over the Chicken Coop restaurants."

"So the Roast Roost wants to take over the Chicken Coops!" Bob said. "Amazing! But why would Argenti try to run Juliet Coop off the road?"

"I don't know," Jupe replied. "Perhaps he was trying to get to Big Barney with a little brutal persuasion."

"Do you think he's the one who's trying to poison Big Barney's chicken?" Bob asked. "I mean, he's our only suspect."

"No—there's still Big Barney himself, and of course Mr. Sweetness, if he ever surfaces again," Jupe said.

Just then the telephone rang in Headquarters. Pete reached it first.

"Three Investigators. Pete Crenshaw," he said, flipping on the speaker phone.

It was Kelly calling from the hospital. She said only three words, but they were enough to send The Three Investigators into top speed.

"Pete," she said, "Juliet's awake."

4

Dr. Jones Operates

THE THREE INVESTIGATORS JUMPED INTO BOB'S VW and raced to the hospital, stopping only three times to make minor adjustments to major parts of the engine.

When they got there, they hurried straight to Kelly and Juliet's room. Now, finally, they were going to get the real story of what happened the night of Juliet's accident. Was someone chasing her? Was her crash an accident? What did she mean when she said someone was poisoning the chicken?

"Hey, Paul, John, and Ringo! Freeze!"

Jupe stopped, his hand on the door handle. The Three Investigators looked around and saw red-haired Elizabeth Lazar calling to them from the nurses' station.

"Sorry, you can't go in," she said, smiling at them. "Mr. Coop's in there with his daughter. And the doctors are examining Kelly. You'll have to wait. But you've got time for a couple of choruses of 'I Want to Hold Your Hand.' "

Bob laughed, but Jupe cleared his throat uncomfortably and walked away.

Five minutes clicked off on the big clock at the end of the hall. Then ten minutes. The waiting was driving Jupe crazy.

He walked over and started fidgeting with a stack of papers on the counter of the nurses' station.

"What's your hurry?" Nurse Lazar said to Jupe. She stared at his chest. "You know, you should wear something with a more positive image."

Jupe was wearing the only clean shirt he could find in his drawer that morning. It said: WHEN IN DOUBT— EAT.

"Actually we're eager to speak with Kelly's roommate, Juliet Coop," Jupe said in his most officious tone of voice. "We want to find out what she remembers about her accident."

"Well, you can forget about that," Nurse Lazar said with a little laugh. "She doesn't remember anything. She has amnesia."

Amnesia! The word hit Jupe in the gut like a ton of bricks. After all this waiting and wondering, the one person who could answer their questions had suddenly turned into a blank tape.

Finally the door to Juliet's room opened and Big Barney came out. He stood half in and half out of the doorway, wearing a purple jogging suit with a little yellow and orange chicken embroidered on the chest.

"Okay, it's settled. I'll see you tomorrow," he said to Juliet. "I'll take you home and you'll forget all about this—I mean, everything will be okay. Don't look so worried. Do I look worried? Of course not. *Ciao.*"

Big Barney smiled and closed the door. But as soon as he started walking down the hall, the smile came off his face. He muttered something to himself as he walked quickly past the three teenagers.

"What'd he say? Could you hear?" Pete asked.

"It sounded to me like 'What am I going to do?' " Bob said.

"Let's go," Jupe said, leading the way into the hospital room.

Twenty-year-old Juliet Coop sat in her bed, propped up with pillows behind her. Her curly black hair looked tousled from sleep, but her big blue eyes were wide open and clear. Her face, however, looked uncertain.

"Hi," Kelly said cheerfully, but she gave Pete a "be careful" look. Jupe and Bob caught it as well. "Here they are, Juliet—the Three Investigators. Life-size, batteries not included, and some assembly required." Kelly giggled. "This is Jupiter Jones, Bob Andrews, and this is my Pete."

"Hi," Juliet said. Her voice was soft but raspy. "I know all about you," she said, looking at Pete.

Pete looked sideways at Kelly, while Jupe managed a shy hello.

Bob smiled and asked, "How are you feeling?"

"Like I've gone ten rounds with a boxing champ," Juliet said. "But nothing's broken, no deep cuts, just bruises and scratches. I'm actually going home tomorrow."

"That's great," Bob said.

Jupe impatiently pushed a chair from Kelly's side of the room to Juliet's bed.

"We've been very anxious to talk to you about your accident," Jupe said.

"Kelly told me. But there's something I'd better tell you first," said Juliet slowly. "I have amnesia."

"You can't remember anything at all?" Jupe asked very precisely.

"The last thing I remember is feeding my cat two mornings ago before going to work at my dad's office. Then I woke up here," Juliet said. "The amnesia's temporary. At least that's what the doctor said. It's pretty common after a big shock. My memory could come back any minute."

"If it doesn't, maybe we can help you track it down," Bob volunteered.

"So you don't remember anything from the day of the accident," Jupe mused. "What do you do in your father's office?"

"I just graduated from college with my business degree," Juliet explained. "So now I'm trying to learn Dad's business. I've been going from one department to another, doing a cost-efficiency analysis on the entire operation."

"Do you remember what departments you were studying last Friday?" Jupe asked.

"I don't," Juliet said unhappily.

"Do you remember having some bad dreams, or talking in your sleep?" Jupe asked.

Juliet shook her head.

"Guys, let's talk outside," Jupe said, motioning for Pete and Bob to follow.

Once they were out in the hallway, Jupe said bluntly, "There's no case."

"Kelly thinks there is," Pete said.

"Kelly's been sitting there for a week with nothing to do but watch television," Jupe said. "She qualifies as a certified hospital-bed potato."

"And she's obviously got a wild imagination. I mean, she's going with you, isn't she?" Bob said, giving Pete a friendly punch in the arm.

"Come on, you guys," Pete said. "Kelly knows things. She always knows what kind of clothes or lipstick and stuff to wear months before anyone else is wearing them."

"Great," Jupe said. "If we ever change our name to The Three Fashion Designers, we'll definitely make her an associate."

Pete scowled at Jupe.

"Pete," Jupe said, trying to be reasonable, "Juliet Coop had a bad accident and she had a bad dream. Now she has amnesia. I can't put those together and come up with a crime, can you?"

But it was Bob who spoke up. "I have to give you a 'maybe' on that," he said.

That caught Jupiter by surprise.

"I'll tell you why," Bob said. "I can see the crash wiping out her memory of the accident. But Juliet doesn't remember anything the day of the accident. Why is the whole day erased? Maybe something else happened."

The answer to that one was not on the tip of Jupe's tongue. He was thinking about it when Nurse Lazar's loud voice stole his attention. She was talking on the phone at the nurses' station.

"You're going to have my job?" she said with a laugh, obviously repeating what the person on the other end had threatened. "Pal, you can *have* my job and I hope you look good in the little white hat." She stamped hospital forms with a red rubber stamp as she spoke. "I'm tired of you calling every half hour asking about Juliet Coop. I've got thirty other patients to care for. You want to know how she is? Come to the hospital."

Nurse Lazar listened to the caller's reply with an angry face. "You want to talk to a doctor? Hold on." She dropped the phone loudly on the desk and walked away.

"Why would someone call so often to check on Juliet Coop?" Jupe asked.

"Because he's worried about her," Pete said.

"Right. But is he worried that she won't make it—or that she *will*? Maybe it's Mr. Sweetness," Jupe said. He cleared his throat.

"Jupe, I know that sound," Bob said. "You're deciding what voice to use."

Jupiter had a flare for acting, and he could speak in lots of different voices and styles.

"The man wants to speak to a doctor," Jupe said, smiling slyly. He picked up the receiver.

"Hello, this is Dr. Jones speaking," he said. His voice was suddenly older—exactly like a thirty-year-old's—and full of know-everything confidence.

"Never heard of you," said the voice on the other end. Smooth voice. An older man, at least middle-aged. A fast talker.

"I just joined the staff," answered Jupe. "You were asking about Juliet Coop, Mr. . . ."

Jupiter was hoping the caller would fill in the blank with his name.

Instead the man asked, "How is she?"

"Well, I'm only supposed to give out that information to the immediate family," Jupe said. "Are you a family member?"

After a pause, the man said, "I'm a friend of the family."

"A close friend?" asked Jupe.

Question and answer. Thrust and parry. Cat and mouse. The mouse ducked into another hole.

"Look, all I want to know is, is she going to be all right?" said the man.

"She has regained consciousness," Jupe said, listening carefully for the reaction on the other end of the line. "She's out of danger," he added.

"Yeah," said the voice. But it didn't sound like a happy *yeah*, or a relieved *yeah*, or even a questioning *yeah*. It sounded very much to Jupiter Jones like a that's-what-you-think *yeah*.

It gave Jupe a bad feeling. "I'll be happy to tell her you called," Jupe said, trying once more to get a name from the caller.

"That's okay, Doc," Jupe said the voice. "I'll be interfacing with her." The man hung up.

"What happened? What's wrong?" asked Pete, impatient with Jupe's silence.

"He stopped interfacing with me," Jupe said, putting the phone back on the desk just as Nurse Lazar returned with a young intern.

"The guy's a real pain," she said to the intern as she picked up the receiver. But the line was dead. "I don't believe it. He hung up!" she said in disgust.

"He's more than a pain," Jupe said softly to his friends. "He's a mystery. Something is going on and I don't understand it."

"Translation: You're not quitting after all, right?" Bob said.

"I never said I *was* quitting," Jupe replied. "I don't know what and she can't remember why, but I think Juliet Coop is in some kind of danger. And we're the only ones who know it. We've got to stay close to her."

But for the time being, they couldn't stay close to Juliet because they each had pressing things to do. Pete, who often did auto repairs for a few bucks, had to finish adjusting the ignition timing on his neighbor's Corvette.

Bob was due again at the talent agency, where he

worked part-time. One of its rock bands needed help setting up for a club date.

And Jupe had promised to check in with Mrs. Teitelbaum, the neighbor who had given him the melon diet in the first place. Mrs. Teitelbaum considered herself to be Jupe's personal one-woman diet support group.

So it was the next morning when two of the Three Investigators got together again. Jupe and Pete met at the hospital because both Kelly and Juliet were checking out.

Kelly was ecstatic to be leaving. Juliet's spirits had improved, too, but her memory still hadn't returned. She sat on her bed, waiting for Big Barney to come and take her home.

"Knowing Big Barney," Juliet said, "he'll probably show up in a gorilla suit, or bring a mariachi band to the hospital. My dad loves jokes, you know."

Ten minutes later Big Barney stuck his head in the door. "Hey! Remember me?" He was wearing a brown jogging suit and he had a fake arrow through his head.

"Dad, I've only forgotten twenty hours, not twenty years," Juliet said. "Of course I remember you. The question is: Did you remember to bring the stuff I asked for?"

Big Barney produced a small suitcase and Juliet opened it. She pulled out a pair of blue silk pajamas and held them up.

"What are these?" she asked.

"Blue silk pants and blouse," Big Barney said cheerfully. "Just like you asked for."

"Wrong closet, Dad." Juliet laughed. "These are pajamas. I can't go outside in pajamas!"

Big Barney pushed his sunglasses onto his forehead and held out the pajamas at arm's length. "Pajamas? . . . Okay, no problem," he said, the gears in his head already clicking full speed. "We just tell people you're late for a pajama party. Hahaha!" His laugh boomed through the hospital.

"No way," Juliet said, shaking her head. "If Mom were still alive, she'd punch you for even suggesting that!"

"Okay, no problem," Big Barney said. He looked Kelly over as she stood by her bed, packing to leave. "How about her? She looks about a hundred and fifteen pounds."

Kelly was amazed. "One fifteen exactly," she said. "How did you know?"

"I know how much a chicken weighs from thirty yards," said Big Barney. "Similar bone structure. I'd say your clothes would fit my Julie."

"Come on, Dad," Juliet said, embarrassed. "I can't do that. Sorry, Kelly. Sometimes he forgets that the whole world doesn't jump when he pushes an intercom button."

"Hey, it's a great idea," Kelly said. "You're welcome to borrow some clothes."

"You're a lifesaver!" Juliet said gratefully. She

closed up the suitcase Big Barney had brought. "Maybe I could borrow some makeup, too? No makeup bag, Dad," Juliet scolded. She hopped out of bed, gave her father a hug, and said teasingly, "Which one of us lost our memory, I wonder?"

"Here," Kelly said, carrying her own suitcase over to Juliet's side of the room. "Take what you want."

"Thanks," Juliet said. "I'll get them back to you."

"No rush," said Kelly.

"Hey, you know what?" Juliet said. "Dad's giving me a welcome-home party in a couple of days. Why don't you all come? It'll be a great party and you can pick up your clothes then, Kelly."

"Sounds great!" Kelly exclaimed.

Jupe also smiled, but he kept it to himself. A party at the Chicken King's house? A chance to observe Big Barney up close and personal? What could be better?

5

The Party Animal

JUPITER JONES SAT ON THE CORNER OF HIS BED AND pulled on his socks. It was the day of the party at Big Barney Coop's mansion and Jupe was nervous. This was going to be a tough assignment. Not because of the investigation—he was looking forward to that. But what was he going to say to people, more specifically, to girls at the party?

He stood up and tucked a bright polo shirt into his chinos. He faced his mirror. Not bad for a slightly overweight, medium height guy with unruly black hair. Wait a minute. Did the shirt look better tucked in or left out? It was stretching rather tightly over his stomach.

Then be began to have an imaginary conversation in his head. He was talking to a girl, the girl he'd like to meet at the party. She was petite and dainty, with short, curly hair.

"You probably haven't noticed me, but I've been staring at you uncontrollably for half an hour," said the imaginary girl with a smile.

"I notice everything," Jupe answered confidently.

"Want some chicken?" she asked, temptingly holding out a plate of Big Barney's best.

"No, thanks," Jupe said, looking into the mirror in his room. "I'm trying to lose a few."

"Gee, I really admire guys who have will power," replied the girl in Jupe's daydream.

She likes me, Jupe thought.

"Are you a friend of Big Barney's?"

"Actually I'm here to see if he's poisoning his chickens," Jupe said bluntly.

The girl's eyes opened wide. "You mean," she said excitedly, "you're a real detective?"

But by the time Jupe had tried on a more flattering shirt, his imaginary date was asking him a really tough question. "Why would someone who's made millions selling fried chicken suddenly decide to poison his own food?" she asked.

"That's a very astute question," said Jupe. "And I'm not sure of the answer. Maybe he's trying to scare off Michael Argenti. Maybe he's poisoning just a small sample of his own birds, so that when Argenti takes a sample, he'll find contamination. Or maybe he's poisoning Argenti's Roast Roost chickens as a counterattack. There are a lot of possibilities."

"You're so smart and logical," said the girl in the daydream.

"And I know judo, too," Jupe added.

"You've probably already got a girlfriend," the girl said.

"Well . . ." Jupe said.

"Hey, Jupe. Are you ready?" asked a voice from behind.

Jupe snapped out of his daydream and saw Bob standing in the doorway. He was wearing a navy-blue and red striped polo shirt and white casual pants.

"Who were you talking to?" Bob asked as they walked to his car.

"Just going over the facts of the case," Jupe answered, his face flushing.

When they arrived at Big Barney's enormous mansion in Bel Air, Pete and Kelly were waiting for them.

"Hope you brought a lot of change," Pete said. "You need bus fare to get from the front door to the pool."

The mansion was a stately forty-room, three-story stucco building with ivy growing on the walls. But that's where any semblance of elegance stopped. Everywhere there were reminders of how the Chicken King had made his millions. Instead of lawn jockeys there were chickens in jockey uniforms. The windsock on top of the flagpole was a rubber chicken. And many of the fat, round shrubs were trimmed into topiary versions of chickens wearing crowns.

The party was being held poolside, behind the mansion. There, two hundred people, young and old, were gathered around a chicken-shaped swimming pool, eating fried chicken, dancing, and having a great time.

"Remember, we're not here just to have fun," Jupe

said. "Especially you, Kelly. Be sure to 'forget' to pick up your clothes from Juliet. That way you'll have an excuse to see her again."

"I know, I know," Kelly said impatiently. "Come on, Pete, let's go find Juliet. And if I catch you having any fun, I'll tell Jupe on you." Kelly laughed as they walked away.

"Why does she take everything I say so seriously?" Jupe asked Bob.

Bob shook his head. "No—why do *you* take everything *she* says so seriously? C'mon, let's look around."

They squeezed their way through the crowd. It seemed to Jupe that everyone had a juicy drumstick or a chicken wing in their hand. They were pointing with them, waving them, even dueling with them. But most of all, they were chewing on them.

"This is torture," moaned Jupe. "When the wind blows in our direction, I can smell all eight of the herbs and spices in Big Barney's secret patented formula."

"Jupe, have some chicken," Bob said. "It won't kill you."

Bob looked at Jupe and Jupe looked at Bob, and they both winced. Maybe it wouldn't kill them, they realized—and then again, maybe it would!

"No, thanks," said Jupe.

"Hi," said a girl. She was about seventeen, with swept-back short brown hair. She had a juicy drumstick in one hand and an empty soda cup in the other.

And she was staring right at Bob. "I've been watching you ever since you came in."

Bob gave her a winning smile and said, "Don't I know you from somewhere?"

The girl laughed. "Now *there's* a new line," she said. "Sure you know me. I'm your mother."

Bob laughed and steered the girl away. "Hi, Mom. Let's go get something to drink and I'll tell you what a wonderful kid I was."

Jupe sat down in a lounge chair and watched Big Barney work the crowd like a night club comedian. Every once in a while his big voice boomed across the pool, drowning out the chatter of all the other party guests.

But suddenly another voice caught Jupe's attention. It was coming from a man standing directly behind Jupe. Jupe casually turned his head. He saw an energetic man in a white suit introducing himself to a blonde young woman who was only a few feet away.

"Don Dellasandro," the man said, handing the woman his business card.

"Peggy Bennington," said the blonde.

"It's nice to network with you, Peggy," Don said.

The more Jupe listened, the more certain he was that he recognized the man's voice.

"I'm doing some market research, Peggy," said Don. "Do you want to taste something that's going to impact on your life significantly?"

"Sure."

Don handed her a small foil-wrapped candy.

Jupe stood up to get a better view.

"Miracle Tastes?" Peggy said, reading the words on the wrapper.

"That's my company and this is my latest," said Don.

Peggy unwrapped the candy. It was a piece of chocolate. Jupe thought it looked cream-filled.

"I try to stay away from candy," Peggy said.

"But this is zero calories!" Don said with a grin. "And that's only half the miracle."

The candy was in Peggy's right hand, which Dellasandro pushed closer to her mouth. "Taste it and enter the twenty-first century." Peggy finally took a bite.

"It's really good!" she exclaimed.

Jupe's tongue was practically hanging out of his mouth. The man noticed.

"Don Dellasandro," the man said, handing Jupe his business card and a candy at the same time.

The candy was smooth and creamy and delicious.

"What do you taste?" Don asked.

"I distinctly taste three things," Jupe said. "Dark chocolate, marshmallow, and mint. No calories? How do you do it?"

"Flavorings," Don replied. "That's what Miracle Tastes is all about. I create flavors. And you did perfectamento at picking out the tastes. I'm glad I interfaced with you."

Jupe's eyes opened wide. He had been so interested

in the delicious calorie-free candy that for a second he'd forgotten about Don's voice—until that moment. But there was no doubt in Jupe's mind. Don Dellasandro was the man who had been calling the hospital every half hour to ask about Juliet Coop! "I'll be interfacing with her," he had told Jupe just before he hung up.

"I don't suppose you've got a card, do you?" Don said. "You're one heck of a taster."

"Of course he doesn't," Peggy Bennington said, laughing at Don. "He's a teenager."

As a matter of fact, Jupe thought to himself, I do have a card. But that was the last thing Jupe wanted to do—give Don Dellasandro one of his Three Investigators cards. He didn't want Dellasandro to clam up just when Jupe needed to ask him a million questions. Like, why had he called the hospital? Why was he being so mysterious on the phone? And what was Don's connection to Juliet or Big Barney?

Juliet came up to them just then and took Don Dellasandro's arm. "Don, I've got to have another candy. You didn't warn me I couldn't stop eating them," she said happily.

Don gave Juliet another piece of candy in the Miracle Tastes wrapper. "This kid is a natural taster," he said, pointing at Jupe.

"Don't steal Jupiter Jones from me," Juliet said. "Jupe and his friends are detectives, and they're going to help me figure out where I was the day of my accident."

Keep your face frozen, Jupiter told himself. Don't let on that Juliet just blew your cover.

"No kidding," Don said, looking at Jupe with narrowed eyes. "I never would have known it to look at you, pal."

Jupe had to find Bob and Pete fast. He had stumbled onto some kind of a clue, although he wasn't sure what it was.

Jupe excused himself and wandered through the crowd, looking for his friends. Near the beak end of the chicken pool there was a cluster of people, and in the middle, towering over his guests, stood Big Barney Coop. Anyone who was six feet six inches would stand out in a crowd. But that wasn't enough for Big Barney. He wore a bright-orange jogging suit with his chicken emblem stitched over his heart.

"And I said, 'I don't know. I'm still trying to figure out why the chicken crossed the road,'" Barney said with a guffaw. Laughter did not just come out of Big Barney Coop. It detonated, and when it did, even though the jokes weren't the funniest, the aftershocks made the crowd roar.

"Big Barney, just what did happen with the whipped cream chicken shortcake?" someone asked.

"What can I say. 1986," Big Barney said. "The world just wasn't ready for an all-chicken dessert. Hey, does everyone have enough to eat?"

"Actually it was 1985," Jupe interrupted. He couldn't stop himself.

Everyone looked at Jupe, including Big Barney.

"That was the year you installed water fountain hoses for washing down little kids after their meals," Jupe said.

"Hey, guy, you're absolutely on the moola," Barney said, walking over and holding out his hand to Jupe.

Jupe shook it and got a joy buzzer blast.

"Turn the page, guy," Big Barney said, putting his arm around Jupe's shoulders. "Go ahead. My life is flashing before my eyes and I'm loving every word of it."

"Well, 1986 was the year you added sugar to the French fry oil and you had live chickens marching in front of your restaurants with picket signs that said 'I'll do anything for Big Barney,' " Jupe said.

"I'm going to adopt this guy!" Big Barney announced to the crowd. "Juliet, you've got a new brother!"

While Jupe and Barney traded Chicken Coop history, Pete and Kelly were talking with Juliet. She was perched near the back of the low-diving board.

"Great party," Kelly said. "What a crowd. Who are all these people?"

"I don't know—just a bunch of people Dad invited," Juliet said. Her shoes were off and she was dipping her toes in the water. "I mean, I'm really confused, and I'm usually just the opposite—super-organized. This memory loss is driving me crazy. People keep coming up to me, saying 'Glad you're better,' and I can't tell if I don't know them or I just don't remember them."

"You haven't seen a tall, ugly guy, maybe wearing an army camouflage jacket?" asked Pete.

Juliet shook her head. "Doesn't sound like my type," she said. "Why do you ask?"

"Oh, Juliet, I forgot to tell you about him," Kelly said. "I call him Mr. Sweetness. He came to your room the night of your accident. I had the feeling you didn't know him, especially since he never showed up again."

A look of real fear crossed Juliet's brow.

"Let us worry about that," Pete said. "Hey, how's your car? I might be able to help you fix it up if it's not totalled."

"My car? Big Barney shipped it off to the junkyard real fast. He wouldn't even let me see it," Juliet said.

"And you still don't remember anything that happened to you that day?" Kelly asked.

"No," Juliet said. "Maybe something will click when I go back to work next week."

That evening after the party, the Three Investigators sat around eating pizza in Jupe's workshop at The Jones Salvage Yard. Jupe tried to stick to his diet by coming up with a compromise: After every slice of pepperoni pizza he ate two pieces of cantaloupe. It wasn't exactly a system Mrs. Teitelbaum would approve of.

"So what if Don Dellasandro called the hospital a lot?" Pete asked.

"It's the way he called, the sound of his voice, what he said," Jupe said, leaning back in his swivel chair.

"Okay, we'll find out more about him," Bob said, swigging a cola. "But what's this about having a date tomorrow?"

"We have a date with Big Barney's chickens," Jupe said. "He practically adopted me at the party. I guess he recognized a true fan. I managed to secure an invitation to visit his research lab and main offices."

"What do you think we'll find? Boxes sitting around marked 'poison'?" Pete asked, licking a piece of pizza cheese off his fingers.

"I don't know what we'll find there," Jupe answered. "It depends on how thoroughly we snoop around."

"It sounds great to me," Bob said. "But—"

"We know," Jupe and Pete said in unison. "Sax Sendler's Rock-Plus Talent Agency comes first."

"Sorry," Bob said. "Good luck, guys."

They finished the pizza, closed up the workshop, and walked outside the big iron gates of the junkyard to Bob's and Pete's cars. The sky was pink, but not for long.

"Look what's parked across the street," Pete said, pointing down the block to a black Porsche convertible. "Sixty thousand dollars on four mag wheels. An awesome machine!"

"But look at the driver—the guy leaning on the hood," Jupe said quietly. "He's wearing an army camouflage jacket. Just like Mr. Sweetness . . ."

For one second Pete froze. Then he took off running down the street toward the man. "Hey, you!" Pete shouted.

Bob and Jupe followed, but the man in the jacket hopped into his Porsche and roared away.

Instantly Pete turned back and headed for his own car. He jumped behind the wheel and zoomed down the street after the Porsche.

"Great acceleration," Pete said out loud to himself as his Scirocco pulled up right behind Mr. Sweetness's Porsche.

But as they came to the first curve and Pete hit his brakes, he suddenly wished that he weren't going so fast—because the brakes were gone. The pedal was pumping nothing but air!

Pete was speeding down a hill at 50 miles per hour, headed straight toward a busy intersection with a flashing red light!

6

Good Gravy!

FOR A MOMENT PETE COULDN'T STOP PUMPING THE brakes. They had to be working! He had checked the brake fluid himself!

But the fact was, the brakes were dead. They weren't gripping at all. And his car was picking up speed on the downgrade. It was only a matter of seconds until he'd go crashing through the intersection ahead. That is, he'd go crashing *through* it if he got lucky. More likely, he'd go crashing *into* another car crossing the intersection. After all—the flashing red light was on Pete's side, telling *him* to stop. And the other drivers had no way of knowing that Pete's Scirocco was totally out of control.

Pete's throat was so tight it felt like there was a whole apple stuck in it, instead of just his Adam's apple. His palms were sweating too.

But that didn't stop him from grabbing for the gearshift knob. He downshifted from fourth to second, hoping the drag on the engine would slow his car down. Meanwhile the black Porsche in front of him skidded into a U-turn, burned rubber, and took off.

The Scirocco slowed down, but not enough. He was only a hundred yards from the intersection. Cars were whizzing through it from the crossroad as if the yellow flasher on their side didn't exist.

Honnnnnnk! A blue Honda beeped at Pete to warn him that he was going too fast.

With his heart pounding, Pete downshifted again, grabbed the handbrake, and jerked the steering wheel to the right.

Instantly his car swerved off the road and into an empty lot where some low condominiums were being built. The rough terrain at the construction site slowed his car down—but it was a cement block, hidden in the tall grass, that brought the Scirocco to a jarring halt.

Pete's chest bounced against the steering wheel, but his seat belt kept him away from the windshield.

There goes the suspension for sure, Pete thought. He took two deep breaths to calm himself. Then he jumped out and lay down on his back with a flashlight to look under the car. Yup—the brake fluid line had been cut. Pete grabbed his keys, slammed the driver's door closed hard, and jogged back uphill in the dusk to The Jones Salvage Yard.

A couple of cans of ginger ale later, Pete's temper was finally cooling down. He and Jupe and Bob sat on chairs outside their trailer office.

"Well, we have now been introduced to Mr. Sweetness," Jupe said.

"He lived up to his name," Pete said. "The creep must have cut my brake line and then stood there just begging for me to follow him. He knew I'd hit that hill too fast if I was trying to keep up with him."

"It's a good thing you're a good driver, or we'd be The Two Investigators," Jupe said.

"Did you hear that?" Pete said, standing up and accidentally knocking over his chair. "I'm a good driver! A compliment from Jupiter Jones! You're a witness, Bob."

"Oh, I was just thinking of the expense of having new business cards printed," said Jupe.

"But seriously, guys," Bob said, "I wonder who Mr. Sweetness is and why he wants us off the case."

"It may be more pertinent to ask, how did he know we were on it?" Jupe said.

"Good point," Bob agreed. "I sure didn't see him at the party."

"And Juliet doesn't know anyone who wears an army jacket," Pete said. " 'Cause we asked her."

"Okay, so he's not a friend of the family," Jupe concluded. "Maybe he's working for someone."

"But who?" asked Pete.

It was a question they slept on that night.

The next morning, an unfamiliar car horn beeped outside Jupe's workshop and the telephone inside rang at the same time. Jupe, who had been up for hours testing electronic equipment with his oscilloscope, answered the phone while he peeked out a window. One mystery solved: The car horn was Pete's. It sounded strange because Pete wasn't driving his Scirocco. He was in his mom's car.

The telephone call was more of a surprise.

"Jupiter, it's Juliet Coop. My briefcase!" she said excitedly.

Jupe was an expert at all kinds of codes, but this one had him totally confused.

"I woke up about an hour ago and started looking everywhere for my briefcase," Juliet said after taking a deep breath. "Up until then, I'd forgotten I *had* a briefcase!"

Now Jupe was excited too. "Your memory is starting to come back," he said.

"That's one way to look at it," Juliet said. "Or you could say I'm just starting to realize how much I'd forgotten. Anyway, the briefcase isn't here at home. And I don't even know why I want to find it so badly. But I think there's something important in it. I feel like there is."

"Pete and I are just on our way to your father's office," Jupe said. "We'll keep our eyes open for it."

"Maybe I left it in my office," Juliet said. "Or in someone else's office. I'd go looking for it but Dad doesn't want me coming in for a few days. Do you think you could try to find out where I was last Friday before the accident?"

That's exactly what I was already planning to do, Jupe thought to himself.

"We'll ask around," Jupe said to Juliet. "But do you have an appointment calendar? It might give us a head start if we knew what your schedule was."

"Sure. It's a beautiful blue morocco leather diary," Juliet said wistfully. "And you're welcome to look in it yourself—if you can find it. It's always in my brief-case!"

Pete started playing his impatient symphony on the car horn again.

"I'll check out every possibility and call you tonight," Jupe said quickly.

"And I'll call you if I remember anything else," Juliet said before she hung up.

By the time Jupe got outside, Pete had the car hood raised and was peering inside the engine. He was like a compulsive dentist who couldn't resist telling every patient he came across to open wide.

"Juliet just called. She can't find her briefcase, which contains something important," Jupe announced as a greeting.

"I'll bet that's what Mr. Sweetness was hunting for," Pete said without looking up.

If Pete *had* looked up he would have seen Jupiter Jones with his jaw wide open. "Remarkable deduction!" Jupe exclaimed. "What did *you* have for break-fast?"

Then they climbed into the car and headed for Big

Barney's corporate office building in the San Fernando Valley. On the way they passed the lot where Pete's car had gone off the road. It was still sitting there.

Pete pulled into a nearby gas station and hopped out to make a phone call. He was phoning Ty Cassey, Jupe's older cousin, who usually hung around the junkyard and ran an informal car repair business whenever he was in town. Right now, however, Ty was sponging off a *different* distant relative—someone who had rented a beach house in Malibu for the summer.

"Ty?" Pete said into the pay phone. "It's Pete. Remember how you said you needed some wheels for the next three weeks? Well, I'll make you a deal. You can use my car if you'll come haul it out of the field where it's stuck."

Once Pete had arranged with Ty to take care of his Scirocco, he revved the engine of his mom's car again and they were off.

As they pulled into the parking lot at Big Barney's Chicken Coop Corporation, Pete and Jupe had to laugh. In typical Big Barney style, the building was a cross between a modern six-story office complex and an amusement park. To drive through the locked visitors' gate, Pete had to announce himself into an intercom system. But it was the same chicken-shaped intercom used at the Chicken Coop drive-thru restaurants. For a joke, Pete ordered two five-piece meals to go.

When the electronic gate swung open, Pete and Jupe drove toward the red and yellow building.

Big Barney had been at work for hours. He greeted them wearing a big smile and a red jogging suit. The first thing he said to Jupe was, "I've got one. What year did we put the carrots in the coleslaw?"

"1987," Jupe said. "Smaller containers, too."

"Didn't I tell you? Didn't I tell you?" Big Barney bellowed to anyone who was listening inside a three-county radius. "You're a nut, guy, but you're my kind of nut. However, you two will have to wear identification tags at all times. We have tight security around here." Big Barney slapped stickers on Pete's and Jupe's backs.

When they checked each other out, they discovered they were wearing KICK ME signs. Big Barney laughed so hard he almost turned as red as his jogging suit. Then he put Chicken Coop visors on both of them.

"What do you want to see first?" Big Barney asked. "My first dollar? I've got it framed and hanging over the fireplace in my office. How about my first wife? I have her hanging over the fireplace in my office too. Hahahahaha!"

"We'd like to see some of the offices, like Juliet's new office," Jupe said, trying to sound casual about it.

"I want to see where the food is made and what kind of stuff goes into it, too," Pete said.

"So you want to meet my mad scientists, do you?" Barney asked, rolling his eyes wildly. "Okay, I'll have them taken out of their cages just for you. And then I want *you*"—he pulled the visor down over Jupe's eyes—"to taste something special." Big Barney started guiding, although it was more like pushing, Jupe and Pete down the hallways. "You're not going to believe this new product. As a matter of fact, *I* don't believe it and it's my invention."

They took an elevator and toured the offices. Whenever Pete and Jupe could get away from Big Barney for a minute, they asked people if Juliet had been there on the Friday of the accident. One accountant said he had seen her that day. But he didn't remember anything about a briefcase. A few other people mentioned that they'd seen Juliet's Mustang in the parking lot when they left work—but there were no other strong leads.

Finally Big Barney took Pete and Jupe down to the basement, to a large scientific laboratory behind locked glass doors. There were warning signs saying KEEP OUT all around the electronic checkpoint entrance.

When Big Barney pushed a plastic card into an electronic box, the glass doors began to slide open. "Repeat after me," Big Barney said, looking down at Pete and Jupe. "I will tell no one about Drippin' Chicken."

"I will tell no one about Drippin' Chicken," Pete and Jupe said.

"Okay, let's get down to business. *Pandro!*" Big Barney's voice boomed and shook the glass walls of the laboratory.

Instantly a squat, burly, bald man with gold wire-rimmed glasses came marching over. He wore a long white lab jacket that had a row of Chicken Coop pins fastened above the pocket like military medals. And he actually saluted.

"Meet Pandro Mishkin," Big Barney said, pounding the man on the back. It was like pounding a mailbox. "You'll never guess where Pandro came to me from!"

I'll bet it was Disneyland, Pete thought to himself. But he played it straight and asked, "Where?"

"The Pentagon," Big Barney answered. "At least his laboratory in Washington was within five blocks of the Pentagon. Close enough."

Actually, the Pentagon is across the Potomac River in Arlington, Virginia, Jupe thought to himself. But he kept his mouth shut.

Big Barney pushed his paramilitary employee forward. Pandro Mishkin shook hands with the Investigators. His hands were clammy and cold.

"Pandro is a flavor specialist, and he's my head of R&D," Big Barney continued, using the abbreviation for Research and Development. "And if he does a really good job, I'll teach him the other twenty-four letters, too. Haha! Pandro, the boys would like an order of Drippin' Chicken."

Pandro looked at Jupe and Pete suspiciously. "Civilians, sir?" he said.

"They're okay, Pandro," Big Barney said. "What

year did we introduce wings on a string? It was right after I saw soap on a rope."

"1985," answered Pandro.

"June 22, 1985," answered Jupe.

"The guy is a walking unauthorized biography. I love him," Big Barney said. "Go get us some Drippin' Chicken, Pandro."

"Yes, sir," Pandro said. He didn't salute this time. But for a moment he did look like he wanted to click his heels together. Then he marched down the hallway toward a laboratory kitchen, using a key to unlock the door.

"What is Drippin' Chicken?" Pete asked after Pandro was gone.

"Picture this," Big Barney said. "A Chicken Coop boneless white meat chicken patty, deep fried, in a golden baked biscuit."

"I can picture it," said Jupe, almost breathlessly.

"Now, what's wrong with that picture?" asked Big Barney.

"Nothing," said Jupe. "Nothing at all."

"Where's the gravy?" asked Big Barney, grinning like a very large child with a secret he couldn't wait to tell.

"You're introducing gravy in a pump?" Jupe guessed.

Big Barney just shook his head. "The gravy," he said, savoring every word, "is *in* the chicken."

Pete was getting hungry. Jupe was absolutely awestruck.

"You get a bucket of fantabulous gravy in every bite of Drippin' Chicken," pronounced Big Barney. "My brand-new top-secret recipe puts a whole ladleful of real down-home gravy right *inside* each boneless white meat chicken patty. The American people won't know what hit them."

Big Barney's last words gave Jupe and Pete a sudden case of chills. They looked at each other. A moment ago they were salivating for Drippin' Chicken. But now both of them were thinking the same thought. Why wouldn't the American people know what hit them? Maybe it was because the Drippin' Chicken was poisoned!

It made perfect sense. Big Barney was bringing out a new product and Juliet was having nightmares. It could be a coincidence . . . but Jupe's radar told him that Big Barney's supersecret Drippin' Chicken was the subject of Juliet's fears. Her words echoed in their ears: "He's poisoning the chicken. Millions will die."

"They're nice and hot!" Pandro called from the laboratory kitchen.

"Come on, guys. I want you to be my guinea pigs," said Big Barney. "I want you to be the *first* to try Drippin' Chicken!"

7

Choose Your Poison

BIG BARNEY LOOKED AT PETE AND JUPE EXPEC-
tantly. Did they realize what an honor they'd been
given?

Pete looked at his watch. "It's not lunchtime," he
said.

"My diet says no fried foods," Jupe said.

"No excuses!" Big Barney bellowed. "The Drippin'
Chicken is hot. You guys got to learn to grab your
chances—'cause you never know when your timer is
going to start beeping, telling you you're cooked!"

There was no way they could get out of tasting the
Drippin' Chicken without seeming very suspicious. So
Jupe and Pete started slowly walking down the hallway. Holding a tray, Pandro left the lab kitchen and
steered them into his office across the hall. Fortunately Big Barney didn't follow them into the room.
Instead, he called Pandro back out into the hallway for
a quick huddle.

Inside Pandro's office, on his modern glass and

steel desk, sat two steaming Drippin' Chicken biscuit-sandwiches.

"They look superb," Jupe said.

"Are you nuts? They could be poison. We've got to lose them. Put 'em in your pockets," Pete said.

Jupe looked down at his blue jeans, which were already a little on the tight side. "Are you kidding?"

"Well, we can't use the wastebasket," Pete mumbled. "They'd find them. And I'm wearing jogging pants without pockets."

"The couch?" Jupe said.

Pete shook his head. "They'd smell them and *then* they'd find them. Your pockets—quick!"

Pete pointed and Jupe obeyed. The gravy oozed out and started running down his leg. "I'll watch the door for Pandro," Pete said. "See what you can find."

Jupe looked around the office for Juliet's briefcase. It wasn't behind or under the desk or in any of the drawers. And the file cabinets were locked. So Jupe switched gears and began looking for anything else of interest.

"Hey, look at this," Jupe said. "Pandro's desk calendar has a page torn off. Six days ago."

"That's Friday, the day Juliet can't remember," Pete said. "And the night of her accident."

"We've got to find out if there's a connection," Jupe said. Just then he heard footsteps approaching. "Be sure to argue with me about the calendar," Jupe whispered to Pete.

Pete nodded. A split second later Pandro strode back into the room. "At ease, men. Good gravy, you two demolished those fast," Pandro said. "You must have really loved our Drippin' Chicken."

"I can honestly say I've never eaten anything like it," Jupe said.

"The General is going to be happy to hear that," Pandro said, referring to Big Barney. "He sends his apologies. Had to go take care of business."

"Did you invent Drippin' Chicken?" Jupe asked.

"No." Pandro shook his head. He sat down behind his desk. "The General went out of house for this one. I told him not to, at first. I said we could handle it right here. But he pulled rank on me and went right to the top. He got Don Dellasandro of Miracle Tastes to develop Drippin' Chicken. I like to say it was the Chicken King and the Flavor King working on the same team."

"So you don't know what's in it?" Pete asked.

"Of course I do," Pandro said. "It was my job to analyze the secret gravy recipe and make certain it contained just exactly what Mr. Dellasandro said it did. Then I gave my personal go-ahead to the General. That's how I got my tenth bird." One of Pandro's stubby fingers pointed to the last silver chicken pin on his lab coat. "But of course it's all classified material. I can't tell you anything else."

"We wouldn't want you to," Jupe said. "Just coming here is exciting enough. After all—we didn't even know Big Barney until *eight* days ago, did we, Pete?"

Pete looked at Jupe blankly. Then he saw that Jupe's eyes were on the desk calendar. "You mean *six* days ago, don't you, Jupe?" he asked with a smile.

"Eight days," Jupe said, shaking his head.

"You're wrong," Pete said, walking over to Pandro Mishkin's desk and flipping the pages of the desk calendar. "It was six days ago. Last Friday. I'm sure of it—hey, the page is missing."

"I know," Pandro said. His voice was automatic, as though he already knew what he was going to say. "I always write my grocery lists on the calendar and take them with me."

"Well, we won't take up your time any longer," Jupe said. "We've got to get home and change our clothes."

Pete started choking and coughing to cover up a laugh. But Jupe was right. The gravy stain on his pants pocket was starting to spread and show.

They found their way out of the office complex and headed home. The Drippin' Chicken went into the nearest trash can.

That evening cartons of Chinese food were stacked like the Great Wall of China in Jupe's workshop. Pete, Jupe, and Bob were having a six-course conference about the case, filling Bob in on everything they'd seen and everyone they'd talked to at the Chicken Coop Corp. that afternoon.

"Well, it sounds like maybe we know the 'what'— the probable poisoning target is Drippin' Chicken," Bob said. "At least that's our best guess up to now. But that still leaves four questions: who, where, when, and how? And there's still the possibility that Michael Argenti is up to something weird."

"We didn't find Juliet's briefcase, so we still don't know what that has to do with anything," Jupe said, rolling up and eating fat pancakes stuffed with moo shu pork and honeydew melon.

"No one even remembered seeing Juliet last Friday—except one old guy," Pete said. "And he wasn't too swift. I bet he was remembering a totally different day."

"Where'd we get this food?" Bob asked suddenly.

"Usual place," Pete said. "Sun Yee Chinese Deli. Why? What's wrong?"

"I'm not crazy about their fortune cookies," Bob said, staring hard at the small paper fortune in his hand. He passed it over to Pete and Jupe.

On the paper was a handwritten message that said:

The food you've just eaten could have
been poisoned. Next time it will be!
Stay away from the Chicken King!

8

A Word from Our Sponsor

JUPE FINISHED READING THE THREATENING FORTUNE cookie message and passed it back to Bob. No one said anything for a moment. They just sat there feeling watched . . . and very vulnerable.

Then Jupe grabbed the other two fortune cookies. The same message was inside all three.

Bob pushed his carton of shrimp fried rice to the far side of the table. "Nothing like a death threat to ruin your appetite," he said.

Pete reached for the telephone.

"Who are you calling?" Jupe asked.

"Sun Yee's restaurant. To find out who did this."

"Good idea," Bob said.

"No, it isn't," Jupe countered. "Don't bother, Pete."

"Why not?"

"Because I'm certain I know what happened," Jupe answered slowly. But he didn't go on.

"Well?" Pete said finally. "What's your theory, Jupe?"

"Well," Jupe said reluctantly, "I think a waiter at the restaurant probably stuffed that message in the cookie. And he probably did it because someone came into the restaurant and paid him five dollars to help out with a little practical joke."

"How do you know?" Pete asked.

"I know, that's all. Trust me," Jupe said.

"Of course we trust you," Bob said. "It's just that—"

"—we know you too well," Pete said, finishing Bob's sentence. "So, like, we know when you're hiding something."

"Okay, okay," Jupe said. "I know the setup with the fortune cookies because I've done it sometimes myself—for a joke, of course."

"So *that's* why your fortunes always say things like 'You are brilliant, handsome, and a leader,' while ours always say 'Try harder to be like your intelligent friend'! " Bob said.

"Oh, brother!" Pete exclaimed, throwing his crumpled-up napkin at Jupe's chest.

"It was just a joke!" Jupe insisted. "There's no similarity between my occasional humorous pranks and this . . . this . . . death threat." Jupe was quiet for a moment while those last words sank in. "The salient point," he went on, "is that this message is the *second* warning we have received. It tells us that Pete's cut brake line was not just an isolated incident—that it was probably related to our investigation into the

Chicken King. Something sinister *is* going on. And we'd better be on our guard from now on, because someone is watching us."

"I'll bet the guy who did this wears army fatigues and drives a black Porsche convertible, right?" Pete asked.

"I wouldn't be surprised," Jupe said. "He certainly knows a lot about us."

The phone rang just as Jupe finished his sentence. It startled all three of them.

"The Three Investigators. Jupiter Jones, founder, speaking."

"Just the badger I want to talk to!" boomed the voice on the other end. "You have the honor of talking to Big Barney Coop!"

"It's Big Barney," Jupe said with his hand over the receiver.

"What's he calling about? Does he know about the Chinese food?" Pete asked.

Jupe shook his head and motioned for Pete to be quiet.

"Listen, guy," Big Barney said into the phone. "I've got big news with a capital Big. Tomorrow yours ever so truly is taping the first Drippin' Chicken TV commercials. I'm talking landmark Chicken History. I want you there, guy. Can't do it without you."

Jupe couldn't believe his good luck. Big Barney was issuing an invitation to do exactly what Jupe wanted to do—hang around and see what Big Barney was up to.

"Where? And when?" Jupe asked.

"Maltin Mix Studios on Alta Vista Drive. One o'clock. I like my team on time."

Then he was gone.

Late that night, after Pete and Bob had left, Jupe watched a videocassette he had made of Big Barney's TV commercials. Barney always sat at a cluttered desk in what looked like a combination office, library, and game room. Sometimes he interviewed guests or read fan letters. But Jupe's favorites were the more unpredictable commercials. Like the time during Big Barney's "Hate a Hamburger Week," when Big Barney threw a whipped cream pie in a cow's face. Or the time Big Barney sat with his back to the camera during the entire commercial because he was angry at the audience for forgetting his birthday.

But Jupe's absolute favorite was the commercial Big Barney made to promote his two new styles of chicken—Cracklin' Crunchy and Burning Barbecue. Big Barney paid a Las Vegas minister to perform a quickie wedding ceremony for two chickens! The picture of one chicken dressed in a tuxedo and the other in a lace wedding dress, with Big Barney standing there as the best man, said just about everything there was to say about Big Barney.

After watching the tape Jupe went to bed, but he spent a restless night. He couldn't stop wondering whether Big Barney was the person whom Juliet had been talking about in her sleep. And was the Drippin' Chicken the product he planned to poison? Or was it something else? Was Big Barney really going to make a commercial to promote a product that could kill millions?

At one o'clock sharp the next afternoon, Bob and Jupe arrived at Maltin Mix Studios just outside of Beverly Hills. Two minutes later, Pete and Kelly pulled up in Kelly's mother's car.

"Look at that," Bob said to Jupe. "You've been complaining all the way over here about not having your own car. But when Pete, of all people, doesn't have a car, what can you expect?"

"Okay," Jupe replied. "I'll stop complaining until Pete gets his car fixed. Then I'll start again."

When they got inside, Juliet met them at the entrance to studio A, wearing a Chicken Coop visor over her curly black hair.

"Hi. Dad's been asking about you," she said to Jupe with a smile. "Have you found out anything new?"

"No," Jupe said. "But according to a fortune cookie we got last night, we're on the right track."

"Good," Juliet said. "I hope you find my briefcase soon. I still can't remember what's in it. But I *want* it! It's becoming an obsession."

Then she took Jupe, Bob, Pete, and Kelly into the glass production booth at one end of the studio, where they could watch the taping. Lots of people from Big Barney's office were there, including Pandro Mishkin, the flavor specialist.

The desk on the set for Big Barney's commercials was piled high today with letters, empty Styrofoam coffee cups, rubber chickens, crayon drawings of fried chicken sent in by a class of third graders, and a photo of Juliet as a child in a Halloween chicken costume.

Finally the director called over the PA microphone, "We're ready. Could someone go get Big Barney out of makeup?"

A minute later Big Barney made his entrance, wearing a jogging suit with alternating red, white, and blue stripes. On his face he wore a rubber chicken beak which covered his nose and upper lip. He carried with him a large antique silver tray with a heavy, ornate silver lid. He squinted against the bright lights, trying to see into the booth.

"Is my guy here?" he called.

"He's here, Mr. Coop," the director said, looking back from his swivel chair at Jupe. The Investigator was wearing his official Big Barney 10 Year Anniversary T-shirt. It had a drawing of a chicken's body with Barney's head.

"Pandro said you went creamed corn over the Drippin' Chicken sample," Big Barney called out. "I've got plenty for everybody today."

"Too bad you wore your good pants," Pete whispered to Jupe.

Once Big Barney was seated comfortably with his feet on the desk, the studio settled down and the director announced, "Quiet please. Drippin' Chicken. Take one!"

And Big Barney began to talk, looking into the

camera as if he could see through it to the people watching TV.

"Hey, guy," he said. "This is your friend and mine, Big Barney Coop. You know that I don't make commercials unless I've come up with some new way for you to make me rich. Well, this time I've got to tell you that I've outdone even myself. Okay, I wasn't there when they invented the wheel. And I wasn't there when they invented penicillin. And I wasn't there when they invented the paper clip. History didn't call me at those momentous moments. Or if it did, I didn't get the message, which is why I'm firing my secretary. Hahahaha! But today you and I are not only going to make history, we're going to eat it."

At that point, Big Barney uncovered the silver tray to reveal a mountain of steaming-hot Drippin' Chicken biscuit-sandwiches. Even the crowd in the production booth began to ooh and aah hungrily.

Big Barney picked up one of the sandwiches and brought it close to his mouth. The camera moved in for a tight shot. The Three Investigators gulped. Was he really going to eat one?

"I have done what people have been trying to do since the dawn of civilization—or maybe the sunset of civilization. I have created Drippin' Chicken, the chicken with a bucket of unbelievable, irresistible gravy in every bite. And get this—the gravy is *inside* the sandwich! That's right. Now there's nothing to get in the way of your having major gravy stains down the front of your shirt. I told my guys, this time let's give people something they never expected in their sandwich. Well, we've done it, and I can't wait for you to gobble it down. Like this!"

Then he did it. Big Barney took a big bite out of the Drippin' Chicken sandwich he was holding. And with gravy dripping down his chin, he gave the camera a big smile.

"Cut," yelled the director. "Great!"

Some of the bright lights in the studio dimmed and people in the booth relaxed.

Kelly leaned over and said to the Investigators, "That was hysterical!"

But Jupe, Pete, and Bob were still watching Big Barney through the studio glass. And they saw him spit out the bite of Drippin' Chicken without even chewing it!

It was as if Big Barney were confessing that Drippin' Chicken was poisonous—too poisonous to be eaten by any human being!

9

Fowl Play

JUPE KNEW ENOUGH ABOUT THE TELEVISION BUSI-
ness to know that the taping session for Drippin'
Chicken wasn't over yet. But he didn't expect it to go
on for another five hours. Big Barney did the commercial twenty times more. And at the end of each
take Big Barney took a big, squishy bite of Drippin'
Chicken, which he promptly spit out when the director yelled "Cut."

When it was all over, Big Barney yelled, "Let's
party!" and invited everyone in the studio to dig in and
enjoy the Drippin' Chicken samples. There was a
microwave off to one side so the samples could be
heated up. The camera crew, floor crew, and production people in the booth all rushed up to pig out on the
hot biscuits filled with chicken and gravy.

Jupe watched carefully.

No one was dropping dead. No one was writhing
with stomach cramps or chills or any of the other
symptoms of poisoning. The only moans Jupe heard

were the sounds of ecstatically happy people raving about the delicious taste.

Slowly Jupe walked over to the desk where the Drippin' Chicken sat invitingly on the silver tray. There were only two sandwiches left. Just as he reached for one of them Bob poked him on the shoulder. "Notice who's not eating the samples?" he asked.

Jupe looked around.

"Big Barney and Mishkin," Bob said. "Why is it the two people who know the most about Drippin' Chicken are the two people who aren't eating it?"

Jupe hesitated—and lost his chance.

"Excuse me," said a young woman. She reached in front of Jupe and grabbed both sandwiches. "I was going to take one to my boyfriend, but they're too irresistible." She gobbled up both of them right in front of Jupe's face.

Jupe gave Bob a look of pure frustration, but he maintained a calm and rational voice. "Oh, well. If it turns out that they're not harmful, I'll have plenty of opportunities to try them fresh from the Chicken Coop."

When the party started to wind down, the Three Investigators ducked out for some fresh air. They leaned against their cars, waiting for Kelly and Juliet and deciding what to do next.

Finally Kelly and Juliet came out of the studio and into the parking lot. Kelly was brushing her long brown hair as they walked. "I'm going with Juliet to pick up the clothes I left at her house," Kelly said.

Jupe didn't like that. He still wanted Kelly to have a reason to keep in touch with Juliet. When he thought Juliet wasn't looking, he shook his head at Kelly. She must have gotten the message because she gave him a small wink and a nod before she got into Juliet's car.

"There goes the Chickenmobile," Pete said. He pointed to a specially built yellow and orange Cadillac convertible with a giant three-dimensional Chicken Coop emblem on the hood. Big Barney beeped the horn as he drove off. It played a cock-a-doodle-do.

"Where's *he* going?" Jupe asked.

"Maybe he's just going to dinner," Pete said.

"Sneaking off to McDonald's?" Bob joked.

"You follow him, Pete," Jupe said, giving orders as usual. "Bob and I will tail Pandro Mishkin. If we're lucky, one of them will lead us to something useful."

Pete drove away in Kelly's car. Bob and Jupe climbed into Bob's VW to wait for Pandro Mishkin to leave. After a while Pandro got into a long Lincoln Town Car, which had a Chicken Coop logo painted on the side, and drove away.

Bob and Jupe followed him for several hours, first to a seaside restaurant where Mishkin had dinner alone, and finally to a small house set back on a very steep hill in an area called Sugarloaf Canyon. It was getting dark by the time they arrived. Sugarloaf Canyon looked like a community planned for people who hated to have neighbors. The houses were hard to get to and set very far apart.

Jupe and Bob parked down the hill from Mishkin's house, wondering what their next move would be.

"Look—he didn't go inside," Bob said as they watched through the thick bushes that surrounded Mishkin's large house. "He's walking around to the back."

"Let's go," Jupe said, climbing out of the Volkswagen with relief after so much time in the cramped car.

They waited a minute to let Pandro get ahead. Then they walked up his long driveway and past the low stucco house, following the path he had taken. All the lights in the house were dark, but at the back they saw an outdoor light shining down from a tree.

"There's a fence," Jupe said. "And from its style and height, I would surmise that there's a swimming pool behind it."

No sooner had Jupe made that pronouncement than he and Bob heard splashing sounds.

"Come on, baby, you can do it," said the familiar voice of Pandro Mishkin. "Come on, my little Petunia. Hup, two, three! Swim!"

More splashing sounds wafted through the soft summer air. The light on the tree cast an eerie glow as it shone through the slots in the wooden fence.

"Who's he in there with?" Bob wondered out loud. He and Jupe looked at each other, puzzled.

"Shall we find out?" Jupe asked softly.

Bob nodded and the two of them approached the gate to the pool area. They opened it noiselessly and slipped inside. A small outdoor shower and equipment house blocked their view of the deep end of the pool. Jupe led the way as they crept around the structure to get a better look.

But suddenly Jupe's foot got caught on a plastic hose. He fell with a loud crash onto a poolside deck chair. One instant later, Jupe and Bob found out who Pandro Mishkin's swimming companions were. Terrible barking, growling, splashing sounds erupted— and two huge Dobermans leaped out of the pool!

"Charge! Enemies in the camp!" Mishkin yelled from the pool. "Sic 'em, Petunia! Get 'em, Zeus! Don't take any prisoners!"

Jupe scraped his hands scrambling up to escape the frantic Dobermans. He stumbled desperately toward the gate. Bob was way ahead of him. They ran as fast as they could, screaming for help the whole time. But who was going to hear them? The neighbors were miles away.

The barking got louder and louder. Where was the gate? Had someone moved it? In reality, it was only a few feet away, but Bob and Jupe felt like they'd been running forever.

Finally Bob and Jupe reached the gate. They ran through it and Bob slammed it shut, locking the dogs inside. But he and Jupe kept running, down the driveway to Bob's car.

"Close one," Bob said, jumping behind the wheel.

Bob peeled away from Mishkin's house so fast that even his little VW kicked up some stones. Jupe's heart was still racing when they were several miles down the road.

Finally Jupe caught his breath long enough to start acting like himself again—which meant analyzing the situation and giving orders. "We didn't learn much," he said. "But we did find out that Mishkin has fairly tight security at home. I wonder why? Let's get back to Headquarters. We have some plans to make."

Later that night in Jupe's workshop, he and Bob told Pete and Kelly about Pandro Mishkin and his swimming Dobermans.

Then it was Pete's turn to report. "I followed Big Barney to a takeout salad restaurant called Veg Out. He bought a chef's salad, took it with him, and drove to Don Dellasandro's office building."

"Miracle Tastes?" Jupe said.

"You got it," Pete said. "Dellasandro's got a building with offices, labs, and a warehouse down in Long Beach."

"How's the security?" Jupe asked.

"The guards look harmless," Pete said. "But the security system on the entrance is a monster. Lots of alarms and a computer keypad to get in."

"Well, I was a real klutz about handling my assignment," Kelly said with a laugh. "Just as Juliet was giving me back my clothes, somehow, just by 'accident,' I managed to spill my iced tea all over them. Juliet felt so bad, she offered to have them dry cleaned herself. I can pick them up at her house tomorrow."

"Or perhaps the next day, or the next," Jupe said,

smiling. "Good work, Kelly." Jupe's head suddenly turned toward the front door of the workshop. He put his finger to his lips and motioned for Pete to follow him. They moved quietly and took positions on each side of the door. Then Jupe opened the door with a jerk.

Outside in the dark there was no one, but there was a box. It was about the size of an extra-large shoe box. It was wrapped in plain brown paper and tied with a red string, and it was lying right in front of the door. The handwriting on the paper said "For Jupiter Jones." Pete scooted the box with the toe of his sneaker, pushing it farther away.

"Feels heavy," he said.

Jupe bent down and picked up the package. "It *is* heavy," he said.

"You going to open it?" Bob asked as Jupe carried it into the workshop, leaving the door open.

"Don't," Kelly said, holding Pete's arm.

Jupe listened carefully for a minute, first to the box and then to the sounds in the night air. Was someone still out there? Pete and Bob listened, too, and their leg muscles tensed, ready to spring into action.

Finally Jupe untied the string. The box seemed to move in his hands. "Whatever's in here is moving around, because the balance of the box keeps changing." Jupe unwrapped the brown paper. But he was holding the box with the lid facing down, so the contents spilled out onto Jupe's feet.

Splat!

Kelly screamed and Jupe's face went white.

There, lying on Jupe's new white sneakers, was a dead chicken—with its head cut off! It was floppy and freshly-killed, with a big smear of blood at the neck. Then Jupe saw the note, also stained with chicken blood. Slowly he picked it up. It said:

> Jupiter Jones—
>   You're already plump enough to be
>   slaughtered. Stay away from things
>   that aren't your business! This is
>   your last warning!

10

Just Us Chickens

BOUNCE . . . BOUNCE . . . BOUNCE . . . IN THE warm morning sunshine, Pete dribbled around Jupe and made a break for the basketball hoop above his garage door. He went up for a back-handed lay-up and all 190 pounds of him stuffed the ball through the net.

"Come on, Jupe," Pete said, passing the basketball back to him. "Are you playing?"

"I keep thinking about last night and that chicken," Jupe said.

"You're telling me," Pete said, coming up to Jupe. "Yuck—it's enough to give us nightmares for a week. That's why you've got to get some exercise. It'll take your mind off having to wash all that blood off your shoes."

Jupe gagged, remembering the horrible sight of the headless chicken, dripping blood and veins. While he was trying to catch his breath, Pete knocked the ball out of his hands and went in for another lay-up.

"Let's not relive the moment," Jupe said with a

shudder. "The question is, who sent it? Who wants us to stay away from Big Barney? It doesn't seem like the kind of thing Big Barney would do himself. He's giving us other signals—inviting us to come closer, to get involved with his business."

"Jupe," Pete said seriously, "you'll figure it out. You always do. I have faith."

Jupe smiled at his friend and quickly stole the ball from him. Jupe threw a long, arching shot toward the basket—and missed by a mile.

"You're getting closer," Pete said. "You're definitely in the same state."

Bob's car horn beeped in the driveway and he hopped out as soon as the VW chugged to a stop.

"Morning, guys," Bob said. "Seen the paper, Jupe?" He tossed Jupe the morning edition. "Check out the front page of the business section."

Pete tossed Bob the basketball and they shot a few while Jupe read the news story.

"This is extremely timely," Jupe said a few minutes later. "Michael Argenti has intensified his efforts to acquire the Chicken Coop restaurants. Hmmm . . . I've got to make a phone call." He disappeared into Pete's house.

Five minutes later he came out, wearing the famous Jupiter Jones I-told-you-so smile.

"Who'd you call?" asked Pete.

"Michael Argenti," Jupe said. "I thought it was time that we checked him out. After all, it's possible that he won't succeed in buying the Chicken Coop restaurants. In which case, he might settle for merely ruining Big Barney's business by poisoning his food."

"What'd Argenti say about that?" asked Pete.

"I didn't talk to him," said Jupe. "His secretary said he was out of town today. And do you know where?"

"No, but you'd better know or this is a really dumb conversation," Pete said.

"Petaluma," Jupe announced. "Just north of San Francisco. It's where Big Barney has his chicken farms."

In less than an hour Jupe and Pete were climbing aboard a commuter plane to San Francisco. They had phoned Juliet and gotten her to agree to pay all their expenses in this investigation—although she didn't realize that they were also investigating her father. Bob stayed behind because he had some heavy-duty responsibilities at the talent agency. One band was scheduled to play at two different weddings that day, and Bob was supposed to make sure that the band didn't get too drunk to make it to the second wedding reception on time.

At San Francisco International Airport, Pete and Jupe rented a car and drove an hour north to Petaluma. They had no trouble finding Big Barney's ranch. It was well marked and well known to everyone in town.

The ranch itself looked more like an automobile factory than a chicken farm. There were two huge cinderblock buildings, each two stories high and about as long as a football field. Surrounding them was a chain-link fence.

Pete and Jupe stood outside the fence for a moment and stared. Maybe because it was Saturday, no one was around. So the guys opened the gate and walked fifty yards to the first building. A quick check to see if anyone was watching—then they sneaked inside.

They couldn't believe their eyes—or their ears. Inside they saw not hundreds of chickens, but hundreds of *thousands* of them in a well-lighted space. The noise was incredible. Light poured in through a greenhouse-style glass roof, but air conditioning kept the temperature down.

Jupe and Pete grabbed two Chicken Coop visors that were hanging on a peg by the doorway. They put them on so they'd look like employees and started to snoop around.

The first thing they found out was that it was very difficult for human beings to move in this building. Besides the countless chickens, there were long red plastic pipes mounted a few inches from the floor— and they were everywhere. The pipes ran the entire length of the building, like long, low hurdles. Pete and Jupe had to step over them to walk around. These were feeding pipes, with small red plastic bowls attached every eighteen inches. There were also water pipes, with small purple nozzles for the birds to drink from. The entire process of chicken raising was automated, which was why no people were around.

The birds were grouped into long sections according

to age, from little purple fuzzy chicks up to fat, full-grown, bright-plumed birds. Pete and Jupe walked from section to section.

"Why do some of them look so strange?" Pete asked. "Look at that guy—he's got the weirdest little wings I've ever seen."

"Genetic engineering," Jupe said. "A process of planned nutrition and selective breeding so that desirable physical and biological traits become dominant. Some are bred so their wings are big and some so they have big breasts to produce a lot of white meat. That's why that one looks top-heavy, like it's going to fall over."

Suddenly Jupe and Pete saw they were not the only humans in the building. Three men had entered and were looking around. They were standing where Jupe and Pete had come in, among the smallest chicks.

"Quick," Jupe said. "Look busy."

"There's nothing to do," Pete said. "Everything's done by machine."

"Then hide!"

Jupe and Pete ducked down behind a partition that separated one breed of chickens from another. It was a low partition, and they could see over the top of it to watch and eavesdrop on the men who had come in. But the chickens were crowding around them, pecking at their legs.

"I've got to get out of here," Jupe said, suddenly feeling claustrophobic. "Every time I see the white ones, I remember that package we got last night."

But just then the three men moved closer to the guys. One of them wore a red plaid shirt and khaki pants. His white cap, with the Chicken Coop emblem on it, said HANK in big red letters. The other two men looked totally out of place. They wore dark blue suits, and one had mirrored aviator sunglasses. He was young, with short dark hair. When he removed his sunglasses, his blue eyes were like the flames of a blowtorch.

Then Jupe heard Hank say, "Anything else I can show you, Mr. Argenti?"

Michael Argenti? This was one conversation Jupe had to hear!

Michael Argenti looked right through Hank and talked only to the other blue-suited man. "I've seen enough," he said in a dissatisfied tone of voice. "Make some notes and write up a memo. I'm going to have to make some real changes around here. I can see that."

"Yes, Mr. Argenti," said the eager assistant, digging out a pen and small notebook from his jacket pocket.

Michael Argenti put his mirrored sunglasses back on and looked at Hank. "What's your output?"

"From hatched egg to slaughter in nine weeks," Hank said. "We get fifty thousand full grown about every week."

"Not enough. The population's got to be doubled," Michael Argenti said.

The assistant wrote that down.

"Big Barney doesn't like the birds too crowded," said Hank.

"This isn't a rest home for chickens," said Michael Argenti with a nasty smile. "It's a factory. The more units we turn out, the more money we make. At Roast Roost we get mature birds in seven weeks. You're going to have to be that good, too."

Michael Argenti looked around the plant again, shaking his head. Then he bent down and took a handful of grain out of one of the feeding bowls. Little chicks pecked at it in his open palm. Michael Argenti looked back at Hank. "The feed's gotta change, too. But I'll take care of that personally," he said. "I've got something special in mind."

By that time, the assistant had the door to the outside standing open. Michael Argenti walked through it and climbed into a stretch Mercedes limo without breaking his stride. As the car drove off Jupe read its license plate.

It said PLUCKER-1.

11

Bumper Cars

"**W**ELL, MICHAEL ARGENTI WAS EVERYTHING I EX-pected him to be," Jupe said to Pete as they drove south, heading back toward San Francisco. "A brash, arrogant, ruthless, self-important business animal."

"Just what I was thinking," Pete said. "But you left out the word 'jerk.' "

They rode in silence for a while, but around 7:00 P.M., when they were just a few miles outside of the city, Jupe suddenly yelled at Pete, "Pull over!"

"What's wrong?" Pete asked as he steered their small rented car onto the highway off-ramp. Then Pete saw the sign. It was a tall painted chicken with a flashing neon crown, perched on the purple barn roof of a Chicken Coop restaurant. "What happened to a melon a day keeps the pounds away?" Pete asked.

"There have been a number of scientific studies lately which have hypothesized that foods rich in saturated fats may actually be beneficial to people," Jupe said.

"That's barn crud and you know it," Pete said. "But so is your melon diet. So let's eat!"

Pete parked the car and caught up with Jupe, who was not wasting a second getting into the Chicken Coop restaurant.

Jupe stopped at the doorway, inhaling deeply. "Did you know that the sense of smell is one of the weakest of the five senses?" he told Pete. "After you've been in a particular aroma for even a short period of time, you become dulled to it and can't smell it anymore. That's why it's important to savor that first blast of grease when you walk in the door."

"Give me a break, Jupe. People are waiting behind us to get in," Pete said.

They walked to the order counter, where a teenage girl in a purple plaid shirt and a khaki skirt stood smiling at them. She wore a white cap that didn't have a bill. It had a beak. According to the purple writing on her hat, her name was Carly. Carly gave them the official Big Barney greeting.

"Hi there, buddy. Hi there, friend. It's great to have you back again," she said. "What's your order? What's the scoop? We've got it from hen's teeth to soup. What would you like?"

"I'll have a six-piece murder to go," Pete said absently.

"Excuse me?" the girl said.

"Oh—sorry," Pete said. "Six-piece chicken."

Then Jupe ordered a full chicken dinner and the two of them found a table by the window. But when they sat down to eat, Pete didn't touch his food.

"You know," Pete said, "we're making a pretty big assumption here. I mean, what if *this* food—that drumstick you're about to demolish—is the stuff that's poisoned?"

"I haven't forgotten and I haven't ruled out the possibility," Jupe said. "But there are times in a man's life when he just has to take a risk—and this is one of them." He bit into the drumstick and closed his eyes to savor it.

Pete shrugged his shoulders and picked at his own food.

"The key to this case is Juliet Coop and, quite possibly, her missing briefcase," Jupe said when he had eaten a few more bites. "Unfortunately, we can't wait for her amnesia to pass to find a solution. Our poisoner knows we're on the case, and if he can't scare us away, he may decide to speed up his plans. So let's consider what MOM has to say about our three suspects."

"My mom would say, 'Don't get into any more trouble, Pete. You've given me enough gray hairs already,' " Pete said.

"Not that kind of mom," Jupe said. "I was referring to that classic formula for all detection: Motive, Opportunity, and Means. Now, as for Big Barney, he certainly has the means and the opportunity to poison his food. He could introduce something into the birds' diet or inject the birds during processing."

Pete looked down at the chicken in his hand and dropped it onto his tray.

"But what is Big Barney's motive?" Jupe went on.

"He's nuts," Pete said.

"Is he nuts enough to kill millions of people and injure his own daughter?" Jupe asked.

"I don't know," Pete replied. "But who else would send you a chicken with its head cut off?"

"Anybody can buy a chicken. And we can't forget that Michael Argenti is in the chicken business too," Jupe said. "*There* is a man with an irrefutable motive. I'd say he's determined to either take over Big Barney's business—or ruin it. If the takeover deal goes through, fine. But if it doesn't succeed, maybe he's planning to poison Big Barney's chickens as some sort of revenge. Maybe his visit to Petaluma today was really a matter of casing the joint to figure out how to poison the feed. That would cover means. And as for opportunity, it seems like anyone has access to Big Barney's ranches. After all, *we* walked right in, no questions asked."

"Okay, how about suspect number three?" said Pete.

"Mr. Sweetness? Your guess is as good as mine. He's fronting for someone—but who?"

They pondered the suspects as they dumped their trash in a chicken's mouth garbage can and then headed for the car.

It was dark outside as Jupe and Pete drove into San Francisco. The famous San Francisco fog had already begun to roll in. It hovered like a doughnut around the two towers of the Golden Gate Bridge, so that the guys could see the tops of the towers and the traffic underneath, but nothing in between.

San Francisco's seven hills were similarly draped in patches of fog, which left the peaks and valleys clear but clouded up the midsections. Pete thought it was awesome and Jupe tried to analyze the meteorological elements that produced fog every night in the middle of summer.

Then they checked out all of San Francisco's rock radio stations, spinning the dial, listening for a cut by the Stone Bananas, one of Sax's new groups.

When they were only ten or fifteen miles from the airport, however, Pete began to get nervous. He kept glancing in the rear-view mirror and drumming his fingers on the steering wheel.

"Take a look behind us, Jupe," he said. "See a purple Cavalier?"

"I see it," Jupe said. "What about it?"

"I think he's following us," Pete said.

Logic said no. No one knew they had come to San Francisco. It was such a spur of the moment trip. But Pete said yes so strongly. "Okay. Slow down," Jupe said. "We'll take a look."

Pete slowed a little more and the purple car moved up on them, switching to the right lane. Now it was almost even with their back right bumper. Jupe turned to look, but the headlight's bright beam prevented him from seeing the driver's face. Jupe rolled down his window. The driver in the purple car rolled down his window and pulled up a little more. Now he and Jupe were side by side, face to face.

Jupe gasped and jerked back away from the window. It was Mr. Sweetness! He was wearing the army camouflage jacket, his arms bulging in the sleeves. His face was somewhat pockmarked and he held his mouth in a frozen half smile, half sneer. Jupe knew immediately that he was staring into the cold eyes of a killer.

"Let's get out of here!" Jupe shouted.

Pete took his eyes off the road long enough to see exactly what Jupe was shouting about. Mr. Sweetness laughed and suddenly the purple car swerved at them. But Pete stepped on the gas and their rental car jerked ahead.

"He's not just following us. He's trying to smear us across the road," Pete said, taking a quick glance at his mirror.

Mr. Sweetness pulled back into Pete's lane and stayed directly behind him. Every time Pete slowed down for traffic, the purple Cavalier lunged forward and hit them. *Ram!* Hard enough to dent the bumper but not hard enough to mash body metal. *Ram!*

"Take an exit," Jupe said. "We'll lose him!"

Pete pulled off the highway quickly, but so did the Cavalier. No matter how fast Pete drove, the Cavalier was always able to keep up. *Ram!* There didn't seem to be any choice but to keep on driving . . . but for how long? *Ram!*

Both guys realized that being so far away from Rocky

Beach had made them feel safe. The idea that no matter where they went, Mr. Sweetness would be there too, had never occurred to them. Now they were facing that reality . . . alone . . . in the dark . . . *Ram!*

When they reached a remote hillside residential area, Pete turned sharply and aimed the car up a hill. *Ram!* A sign indicated that they were taking a scenic route up to one of San Francisco's most famous tourist attractions—Twin Peaks. From the tops of these two mountains, sightseers had a panoramic view of the water, the city lights, and the entire Bay Area.

But as the road curved upward, Pete found that they were driving right into the doughnut of fog ringing the mountains. *Ram!*

"I've never seen fog like this," Pete said desperately, slowing the car. In fact, it was so thick that they couldn't see more than a foot in front of their headlights. *Ram!* For a moment, Pete thought about turning around and going back down the mountain. But there wasn't room—and they knew Mr. Sweetness wouldn't allow it. *Ram!*

Jupe looked nervously out the back. He couldn't see the Cavalier at all. He couldn't even see another set of headlights. But he *felt* it each time Mr. Sweetness rammed into them.

Then, for what seemed like many minutes, nothing happened.

"Do you think he stopped?" Pete asked Jupe in a tense, thin voice.

"I don't know," Jupe answered. "I can't see a thing. Just keep driving."

Pete gripped the wheel even tighter. They were coming to a curve in the road, and Pete didn't want his concentration to break. It was almost impossible to see the road right in front of the car, let alone the edge where the ground dropped away sharply.

Suddenly, just as Pete was nearing the sharpest part in the curve, the purple Cavalier appeared out of nowhere, driving on the left side of the two-lane road. He was swerving from side to side, trying to push Pete and Jupe over the edge!

"Watch out! We're going over!" Jupe shouted.

Pete pulled the wheel to the left, tires squealed, and they felt the car jerk back onto the pavement from the shoulder. Then Pete held his breath and sped forward blindly. No matter how terrifying it was to drive in this fog, it was better than sticking around for another encounter with Mr. Sweetness.

At the top of the hill the fog disappeared. They had driven high enough to be above it.

With his heart pounding, Pete backed into one of the parking spaces in the curved parking lot overlooking the magnificent vista below. His hands shook as he wiped his forehead.

"Now let's just wait for Mr. Sweetness to show up," Pete said in a furious, let's-get-tough tone of voice.

12

Unwrapping a Clue

PETE AND JUPE SAT SILENTLY ON TOP OF TWIN PEAKS with the motor running. They were waiting for the purple Cavalier with Mr. Sweetness in it to burst through the fog to the top of the hill. Now that they were out of the fog themselves, and surrounded by a few dozen sightseers who could back them up, Pete felt less frightened and a whole lot more angry. In fact, he was burning mad.

"The guy's got a lot of nerve," Pete said, hitting his fist repeatedly on the steering wheel. "I'd like to meet him in a fair fight, I'll tell you that." Pete mentally ran through all the karate moves he knew and would use on Mr. Sweetness if he got the chance. "Why doesn't he show up? What's he doing on that road, anyway?"

"I don't know," Jupe said thoughtfully. "There are a lot of possibilities. . . ."

They waited about thirty minutes and still the Cavalier didn't show up.

Suddenly Jupe slammed his fist into the dashboard. "We've got to get to the airport," he said.

"But what about Mr. Sweetness?" Pete said.

"He's not coming," Jupe said. "He probably turned around and went back down the hill."

Pete slapped the steering wheel with his palms and put the car in gear.

"Look on the bright side," Jupe said. "Now at least we know exactly what he looks like."

Pete drove quickly to the airport and pulled into the Rental Car Returns area. They left the keys in the car, as instructed, and then rushed into the rental office to pay. But just before they got to the office, Pete spun Jupe around by the arm.

"Look!" he said, pointing to a returned car parked near the front.

"A purple Cavalier!" Jupe exclaimed. "But is it the one we're looking for?"

They walked over and circled the empty car.

"It's the right license plate," said Jupe. "Quick! Go into the office and see if he's still in there, and stall him. If he's not there, try to find out from the clerks what Mr. Sweetness's real name is. I'll be there to help you in a minute."

As Pete left, Jupe opened the purple car's passenger door and leaned inside. Was there something in the car that might be a clue? Jupe started searching, meticulously checking the carpeting behind, under, and in front of the seats. He checked the ashtrays and the glove compartment, and even squeezed his hand into the narrow space between the pedals to check under the floor mats. Then he stood up, puffing a little from being bent over for so long.

But it had been worth it. He had found something, something crucial. It didn't tell him who Mr. Sweetness was. But it told him the next best thing—where he might go to find out. Jupe rushed to the rental office and met Pete coming out.

"What did the clerk say?" asked Jupe.

"Have a nice day," Pete said.

"About the purple car," Jupe said impatiently.

"Have a nice day," Pete repeated. "That's all it says. It's a computer."

"Look what I found," Jupe said, pulling out a small crumpled piece of paper, shiny foil on one side and plain white on the other.

"A candy wrapper," Pete said, smoothing it until he could read the name written in silver ink. "Miracle Tastes! It's like the candy Don Dellasandro handed out at Big Barney's party!"

"Yes, exactly," Jupe said. "Free samples of a product not on the market yet. This creates two possibilities. Mr. Sweetness could have been at the party and gotten candy samples as we all did. Or—and this would be considerably more interesting—perhaps Don Dellasandro and Mr. Sweetness are in league together."

"We're just a plane ride from finding out," Pete said. "Let's go home!"

It was midnight when Jupe returned to the junkyard and too late to do anything except work on his latest electronic project—the lock combination decoder. When he got too tired to tinker with it anymore, he turned off the workshop light and started to lock up.

Just then the phone rang.

"Hello?" Jupe said in the darkness.

"Hello, Jupe, it's Pete. Kelly wants to talk to you. Tell him, babe."

Jupe flipped the lights back on.

"Hi, Jupe!" Kelly said with an awful lot of energy. "Well . . . like . . . you know, Juliet Coop took me out to lunch today . . ." she began.

Jupe could picture Kelly twisting one long brown piece of hair, and he knew this was going to be a long story. He put the call on the speaker phone so he could walk around while he listened.

". . . but she doesn't remember where she was or where her briefcase might be," Kelly was saying. "But she remembers something about a car behind her that night . . . but it's still fuzzy. Anyway, after lunch she gave me a ride home, and it was great. Big Barney just gave her a new Mustang convertible."

"You know the one," Pete interrupted in the background. "The baby with the five-liter V-8 engine and the—"

"Pete, please," Kelly said. "Jupe wants to hear this story. So anyway, where was I? Oh, yeah. So before she got in the car, she opened the trunk and threw in her purse. Hey, I said to myself, that was weird. So I asked her, 'What'd you do that for?' 'Habit,' she said. She was riding with the top down once in her old Mustang and someone reached in and grabbed her purse. So do you get the picture, Jupe?"

Jupe's eyes lit up. The trunk! Juliet's briefcase might be in her trunk!

"Yes! A brilliant observation, Kelly. You're learning a lot from me," Jupe said.

Kelly sort of snorted a laugh.

"Let me talk to Pete," Jupe said. "Pete, first thing Monday morning, we're going to the auto salvage yard to check out the trunk of Juliet's car."

"Knew you'd say that," said Pete. "Okay, see ya."

At 9:00 Monday morning, Pete and Bob showed up in the VW. But Jupe wasn't quite ready. He picked up the phone and dialed the number of police headquarters. When Chief Reynolds got on the line, Jupe announced he was calling about Juliet Coop's briefcase.

"A briefcase is news to me," said the chief.

"Of course, you searched the scene of the accident thoroughly for all personal property," Jupe said.

"Of course," the chief answered patiently.

"And the car?" asked Jupe.

"Jupiter, I have uniforms that are older than you are," said Chief Reynolds. "I know how to do my job. My guys said the car was empty."

"I was just checking loose ends," Jupe said.

"Grasping at straws, you mean. You wouldn't want to put a little wager on this case, would you, Jupiter?"

asked Chief Reynolds with a laugh. "Loser buys the winner a Big Barney dinner?"

"Chief, if I lose this one, Big Barney's chicken may be the last thing you'd want to eat," Jupe said. "Talk to you later."

Then Jupe joined his friends and the Three Investigators drove over to the Miller Auto Wreckage Yard. It was the size of two city blocks and surrounded by a tall wooden fence. The far side of the yard was piled high with newly wrecked cars just waiting to be stripped. Scattered elsewhere throughout the lot were piles of various sorts: tires, fenders, cars that were too damaged to be used for parts, and so on. In the left rear corner of the lot there was a huge compactor machine and a 200-foot crane.

Almost as if it had been planned by a television action-adventure show writer, they arrived at the exact moment when Juliet's little blue Mustang was being lifted into the air by the enormous electromagnet on the end of the crane.

"He's going to drop it in the masher!" Pete shouted. "It'll squeeze the metal into a solid block!"

"We'll never get anything out of the trunk then," Bob said, breaking into a run.

They ran as fast as they could to the crane, shouting and waving at the crane operator. When they got there, they saw it was Dick Miller, the owner's son, who had just graduated from Rocky Beach High School a year ago.

He shut down the motor and stepped out on the big yellow painted platform around the operator's cage. "What's your problem?" he shouted down to them.

"If that's Juliet Coop's car, we've got to see it," Jupe shouted back.

"That's it, all right," Dick Miller said. "But it's past it for spare parts, guys."

"We only need to inspect it for a minute," Jupe said.

"Okay, I'll set it down over there," Dick Miller said, pointing to a space in the middle of the yard beside a huge pile of trucks.

The Three Investigators nodded and headed for the area where Dick Miller had pointed. As they walked the crane's engine started up again and the wrecked car, dangling at the end of the flat, round magnet, started moving after them. Jupe looked over his shoulder and saw the car swinging gently back and forth. But then it began to pick up speed, swinging in wider arcs.

"That thing's gonna really hit hard when it hits the ground," Pete said. "He's crazy."

They moved back out of the way but the car above them followed, swinging dangerously near.

"What's the joke?" Pete shouted above the roar of the crane's engine.

"It's no joke! Look!" Bob shouted.

On the ground at the foot of the crane lay Dick Miller. He was holding his stomach, doubled over in pain. Someone else had climbed up into the crane operator's booth and was now working the controls. The crane swung the car ten feet above their heads.

"Who's operating the crane?" Jupe asked.

But there wasn't time for an answer. Suddenly the crane swung the car toward them, and then the electromagnet let go of Juliet's car. All 3,000 pounds of mangled metal came falling to the ground.

13

A (Brief) Case for Murder

THE CAR HIT THE GROUND WITH A SHATTERING crash. Fortunately the Three Investigators had dodged just in time. They crouched behind a stack of wrecked cars, watching the empty electromagnet swing freely in space. All by itself, the magnet was big enough and heavy enough to knock a person dead. And it was obvious that whoever was in the operator's booth wouldn't mind that kind of "accident" one bit.

When the giant magnet stopped swinging, Pete peeked out from his hiding place to see who was in the crane's cab.

"I should have known," he whispered to his buddies. "It's Mr. Sweetness."

All three Investigators came out from behind the stack of cars. They saw a tall man in army camouflage fatigues climbing out of the cab of the crane. He jumped down and gave Dick Miller a chop to the back of the neck to keep him from getting up.

"He's coming this way," Pete said, motioning to his friends to back away. The three of them ducked around to the other side of the car pile, trying to stay out of sight.

"He probably wants to get into Juliet's car—just like we do," Jupe said.

Suddenly they heard a bottle break followed by a sharp crackling sound. Pete didn't look out again until he smelled the smoke. When he looked, he saw Mr. Sweetness tossing a second Molotov cocktail into Juliet's car.

"He's destroying the evidence!" Pete said frantically.

"So that's it," Jupe said. "He doesn't want what's in the car. He just wants to make sure *we* don't get it!"

"If there's still gas in the tank, that car will go off like a skyrocket!" Pete said.

As soon as the flames took hold, Mr. Sweetness ran for his Porsche at the entrace of the junkyard. Pete started to follow, but Bob and Jupe held him back.

"Never mind him," Bob said, grabbing Pete's arm forcefully. "We've got to get into that trunk!"

"Quick, before Juliet's car burns up!" Jupe added.

"*Explodes*, you mean!" Bob said.

Pete took one look at Juliet's flaming car and flew into action. He raced around the junkyard, looking in open car trunks and digging through piles. Finally he found what he needed—an old crowbar. Then he rushed to Juliet's bombed-out Mustang. The flames had already eaten away most of the interior and were working their way toward the back—where the gas tank was.

Sweat flew off Pete's forehead as he applied the crowbar to the trunk, all the while keeping an eye on the flames. Finally the trunk lid gave up and sprang open.

"Got it!" Pete called triumphantly as he reached inside and pulled out a soft brown leather briefcase. He waved it in the air for Jupe and Bob to see. "Let's get out of here before this thing blows!" he cried.

Jupe smiled. "Being very familiar with the rules and regulations of junkyards, I know for a fact that gas tanks of wrecked cars are drained," he said to Bob. "The car's not going to blow up."

"Why didn't you tell me that before?" Pete asked, giving Jupe an exasperated glare.

"I knew by the time I'd convinced you it was really safe, the car would have burned up," Jupe said. "You work better when your raw instincts take over."

"Thanks a lot." Pete groaned.

After calling an ambulance, Jupe, Bob, and Pete hung around to make certain that Dick Miller was going to be all right.

"I always heard you guys were detectives," Dick Miller said. "But I didn't know you investigated bombers and stuff like that."

"It's not always this rough," Jupe said with an apologetic smile.

Then they hurried to Big Barney's mansion, where Juliet and Kelly were waiting for them. Big Barney himself was out and not expected home until late.

"Did you find anything?" the two anxious girls said at once as they opened the front door.

Jupe merely held up the briefcase as evidence of the morning's adventure.

Juliet smiled and led the way into the living room, where Jupe laid the briefcase down on the glass coffee table. Eagerly she unzipped the front compartment and pulled out her blue morocco-leather appointment book. She turned to the page that listed her plans for that fateful Friday—the day of her accident, the day that was so blank in her memory.

"Here it is," she said, breathing quickly.

She stared at the page for a minute and then shook her head. "All it says for the whole day is R&D."

"That's Research and Development, Pandro Mishkin's department, isn't it?" Jupe said. "Why would you have been meeting with him?"

"I was spending a whole day in each department, to learn the business," Juliet said. "But I don't remember anything more."

"Maybe you will when you see what else is inside the briefcase," Jupe urged.

Juliet opened the back leather flap and found a three-ring binder with about two hundred xeroxed pages in it. She took it out and flipped through the pages for a few minutes, then dropped it and shrugged. "I don't recognize this material," she said. It was clear that she had been counting on getting her memory of the accident back when the briefcase was found. She was terribly disappointed.

"Do you mind if I have a look?" Jupe said. He picked up the notebook. Pandro Mishkin's name was stamped on the first page. Quickly Jupe scanned the report.

After reading silently for a few minutes, Jupe looked up and addressed the room.

"I believe I can now reconstruct much of what must have happened two Fridays ago, the night of Juliet's accident," he began. "This is Pandro Mishkin's copy of a report about a food additive called Multisorbitane. It was invented by Don Dellasandro several years ago. In the summary it says that Multisorbitane, as a food enhancer, makes foods taste remarkably better and more intense—but there's a catch. It makes food so good, in fact, it's nearly addicting."

"Is that the catch?" Bob asked.

"Surprisingly, it isn't," Jupe said. "The FDA—the Federal Food and Drug Administration—tested Multisorbitane, as it must test all new drugs and products of this nature. But it denied Don Dellasandro permission to market Multisorbitane because it found strong evidence that it might be a carcinogen."

"A what?" asked Pete.

"It could cause cancer," Bob explained.

Jupe cleared his throat and continued. "We know that you met with Pandro Mishkin on the Friday of your accident. And we know that you have his copy of this incriminating report in your possession. Now we move from what we know," he said, tapping the report, "to what we *think* we know. I suspect that you discovered this report, perhaps by accident, sometime during your visit to Mishkin's office. Considering the time of your accident, I'd say it was late in the day when you found it. And when you did, I think it upset you quite a bit," Jupe said.

Jupe was pacing now, going into high gear. "I think it upset you so much that you took it from Pandro Mishkin's office and fled. He probably chased you to get it back. And when you left the Chicken Coop Corp. building in your car, I think that Pandro Mishkin followed you. In short, I believe it was he who was driving the car that left the second set of tracks at the scene of your accident."

"Time out," Pete said. "Why did this report upset Juliet so much?"

"Yes, that is the key question, isn't it?" Jupe said, smiling knowingly. "It upset her because she knew, or suspected, as I do, that Multisorbitane is a key ingredient in a delicious new product called Drippin' Chicken!"

Jupe let them all digest that idea for a moment and then he began again. "You discovered the horrible fact that someone—maybe Pandro, maybe Dellasandro, maybe even your father—was knowingly and quite cold-bloodedly putting this poison into Drippin' Chicken. Of course the effects of the Multisorbitane wouldn't show up for years. But slowly, over a period of time, millions of people who had regularly eaten this carcinogen would begin to get cancer. No one would realize the danger until it was too late."

Juliet's mouth was trembling. "My father wouldn't do something like that!" she cried out.

"We can't really know that—unless you can help us prove it," Jupe said without missing a beat.

It was clear to everyone that his mind, as usual, was working well ahead of the conversation.

"What kind of scheme do you have in mind, Jupe?" Bob asked.

"It's simple," Jupe said. "We've got to find out if Big Barney knows about the Multisorbitane in the Drippin' Chicken recipe. Any idea how we can do that?"

"I know how," said Juliet. "My father keeps the recipes for his products in a safe in his office."

Jupe snapped his fingers. "I was hoping he did. Can you get it for us?"

"I don't know the combination of the safe," she replied. "Only Big Barney knows it."

"Well, that's no good," Jupe said. "We have to get the recipe without Big Barney knowing it. He can't suspect what we're doing."

Juliet suddenly smiled. "How about Dad's secretary?" Juliet asked. "She probably knows more about him than he does. She might know the combination."

"Let's go," Pete said.

"No. I want to go by myself," said Juliet. "I'm not even sure I should be doing this. Dad's recipes are top secret—you'll have to promise . . ."

"Of course, of course," Jupe said. "Now, when do you think we can expect you?"

"A couple of hours," said Juliet.

Two hours came and went. The Three Investigators and Kelly spent the time doing what Juliet had suggested. Eat her food, watch her TV, relax. The third one was too difficult for Jupiter.

Another hour passed.

Finally the door opened and Juliet came in, carrying a piece of paper and giving everyone a large smile.

"I've got the recipe," she whispered, looking around to be sure her father wasn't home. "There's no mention of Multisorbitane in Drippin' Chicken's ingredients. See? My dad isn't some kind of crazed killer."

Jupe grabbed the paper quickly and started reading it.

"Looks like our case is going down the tubes," Pete said.

Jupe folded the paper and put it in his pocket. Then he looked at Juliet. "If no one is poisoning the chicken, then why did you say so in your sleep? And why was it so important to you to find your briefcase? And why was this report about Multisorbitane, with Pandro Mishkin's stamp, in your possession?"

"I don't know," said Juliet.

"We don't know either," Jupe said solemnly. "But there are a few things we do know. For one, our list of suspects is shrinking rapidly. Your father seems to be out. Michael Argenti is out, because we have nothing to connect him with Multisorbitane or with this report from Pandro Mishkin. Pandro himself is a question mark. He could be innocent, he could be involved. But the suspect I'm most interested in is the person who didn't want us to find this report . . . the person who sent Mr. Sweetness to scare us off . . . the person who invented Drippin' Chicken in the first place. Don Dellasandro!"

"What now?" Kelly asked. "Call the police?"

"No. We need proof," Jupe said. "We've got to get into Miracle Tastes and find out exactly what Don Dellasandro is hiding."

"Jupe, the place is a Class A security nightmare," Pete warned.

"Okay, then we'll have to go in there late tonight," said Jupe, "when the guards are half asleep."

"You'd better make that early tonight," Juliet said. "My dad's secretary reminded me of something else I forgot. There's a big press party planned for this evening. Big Barney is going to introduce Drippin' Chicken to the world! Everyone will be eating the stuff."

"Oh, no!" Kelly exclaimed.

Remembering Big Barney's own words, Jupe said, "The American people won't know what hit them!"

14

The Secret Ingredient

AT 5:00 P.M. THE INVESTIGATORS WERE SITTING IN Bob's car, parked inconspicuously across the road from the Miracle Tastes office and warehouse building in Long Beach. They had stopped first at home to change into black jeans and black T-shirts. Jupe also brought with him a small, mysterious black leather case, which he held carefully on his lap. It was something Pete and Bob had never seen before.

"As soon as Dellasandro leaves, we make our move," Jupe said, cradling the black box.

"How do we know he's in there?" Bob asked.

"His car is there," Pete said. "I recognize it."

"When did you see it?" Bob asked, surprised.

"After the taping of Big Barney's new commercial. I followed Big Barney, remember?" Pete said. "And he came here, to Miracle Tastes."

Little by little, the parking lot at Miracle Tastes emptied out. But it wasn't until 6:00 P.M. that Don Dellasandro's gray Cadillac Allanté rolled out and headed up the road toward L.A.

"He's probably going to Big Barney's press party," Pete said.

They got out of the car and ran across the nearly empty Miracle Tastes parking lot. When they reached the entrance, Bob kept watch as Pete and Jupe examined the door.

"Will you look at that security system?" Pete moaned.

All six of their eyes focused on a small electronic panel with a lighted keypad. It was located on the chrome wall beside the glass doorway. Just inside the door was a security guard's station, but no one was there.

"He's probably still making rounds," Bob concluded. "Let's make this snappy."

From the look of the keypad, the Three Investigators decided that it worked something like their own security system at Headquarters. A special combination had to be entered on the keypad before the door would open. But who knew what would happen if the wrong codes were entered?

Jupe unzipped his small black leather case. "Luckily for us, I've been constructing an electronic lock combination decoder for weeks," Jupe said. "Once I connect the decoder to the keypad, my device will read the combination. I've tried it at Headquarters and it works."

Jupe quickly unscrewed the cover plate to the keypad and attached the decoder's two alligator clips to two special wires in the security system. His heart was pounding. He flipped a switch, and after some beeps and flashes the decoder gave Jupe a combination of numbers.

"Okay, let's try it," Pete said, moving toward the door.

But Jupe grabbed Pete's shoulder. "Wait! Something's wrong." Jupe nervously fiddled with the black decoder.

"I'll say it is," Bob agreed when he looked at Jupe's device. "It's giving you the wrong combination. That's the combination of *our* security system at Headquarters!"

Jupe flushed red with embarrassment. "There must be a flaw in the capacitor . . . or the impedence could be incorrectly calculated . . . ahh, I'm sorry, guys."

"Don't worry about it," Bob said. "Just put that thing away—quick! Here comes the guard."

Jupe stuffed the decoder in his shirt and the three of them tried to look casual as the security guard approached the front desk. Before he got there, Bob reached up and rang the night bell.

The guard opened the door only a crack, eyeing them up and down. "What can I do for you?" he asked cautiously.

Jupe was determined to make up for his failure with the lock decoder.

"Three Guys in Black T-Shirts Messenger Service," Jupe said. "We're supposed to pick up something in

Mr. Dellasandro's office. He said it was a matter of life and death."

"It takes three guys to pick up a package?" asked the guard suspiciously.

"Well, I've got the job," Jupe said.

"But I own the car," added Bob.

"And I have a road map," said Pete.

"I thought the Three Stooges were dead," muttered the guard. He opened the door and let them in. "Get your package and get out of here." He motioned impatiently toward a hall.

The Three Investigators followed the guard's directions, taking the carpeted hallway to the left, which led to offices, rather than the concrete hallway to the right.

At the end of the hallway they came to a large walnut door marked EXECUTIVE SUITE.

Don Dellasandro's office was spacious, with ceiling-to-floor windows on two sides. It smelled of fresh-cut flowers, even though there wasn't a single bloom in the room. The central feature of the room was a large rosewood desk with a built-in telephone and computer. There was also Nautilus exercise equipment in one corner. All over the walls were mementos and awards from Dellasandro's past flavoring achievements. Labels from candy bars, salad dressings, babies' rubber pacifiers, frozen mixed eggplant and zucchini, and more were framed and displayed.

The awards didn't impress Jupiter, but the thoroughness of Don Dellasandro's filing system did.

"What are we looking for?" Pete asked, going through Dellasandro's king-size executive desk.

"A jar of Multisorbitane would be helpful," Jupe said, opening another file cabinet. "But I'll settle for any evidence that Don Dellasandro has tampered with the ingredients of Drippin' Chicken." Jupe's fingers flipped through one file folder after another.

"He has a computer terminal in his executive washroom," Bob said from the bathroom, trying a splash of one of Dellasandro's expensive men's colognes. He reappeared in the room. "Does it make me smell like a million?"

"A million what?" Pete asked.

"Brominated pseudophosphates!" Jupe exclaimed.

"Watch your language, Jupe," Bob said. "Pete's at an impressionable age."

"Brominated pseudophosphates is one of the ingredients in Drippin' Chicken," Jupe said. "At least, according to the recipe Juliet got for us."

"It sounds more like something Pete put in my car engine last week," Bob said.

Jupe slammed the file cabinet closed. "But I have just gone through two years' worth of purchase orders, invoices, and inventory lists. There's no evidence that Miracle Tastes has purchased or manufactured any of that ingredient! We've got to get into the warehouse immediately."

They ran back down the carpeted hall and found the same security guard, dozing at the front desk. He woke up with a start. "Get your package?" he asked.

Pete and Bob looked to Jupe to supply an answer.

"No," Jupe said. "He said it would be right here in the warehouse office, but it wasn't."

"Warehouse office?" sputtered the guard. "That isn't the warehouse! Does this look like a warehouse? Don't any of you boys have any common sense?"

"The fourth guy has common sense," Bob said. "But he didn't want to come tonight."

"Go down that concrete hallway. Walk through three red doors. *That's* the warehouse," said the guard. "Do you know what a door looks like?"

"He does," Pete said, pointing to Jupe.

Down the hall, through three red doors, the Investigators found themselves catching their breath in a cavernous room filled with pyramids of sealed drums full of chemicals.

"Spread out and check every label," Jupe said.

"What time is it?" Bob called.

"Almost seven."

"Don't forget the press party starts at nine," Bob reminded them. "We've got to hurry."

Pete and Bob wandered separately up and down the aisles, surrounded by drums of powdered acids.

"Hey, guys, over here!" Bob suddenly called.

Pete and Jupe worked their way through the maze of barrels to reach Bob. Their shoes squeaked on the clean, painted concrete floor. They found Bob standing in front of a stack of barrels. Each one was marked in big letters BROMINATED PSEUDOPHOSPHATES.

"Here's what you're looking for, Jupe," Bob said. "But what does it prove?"

Jupiter examined the barrels carefully. "Look at the received dates on the barrels," Jupe said.

"They came in a couple of months ago," Pete said.

"How could they?" asked Jupe. "I just went through his invoices. They clearly indicate that in the last two years he hasn't ordered or stocked a single pound, a single ounce of brominated pseudophosphates. Let's get a sample out of these drums. I'd like to know what's *really* in them."

"Bottom line? I think you can guess the answer to that question," said a voice behind them.

The Investigators whirled around. Don Dellasandro stood behind them.

"I was hoping we wouldn't have to interface like this," he said. "I was hoping that you'd drop the ball on this investigation, but instead you're impacting on me—negatively."

The guys froze in fear.

"I'm sorry," Don Dellasandro said, drawing a gun from his pocket. He aimed the gun at the Investigators, at about heart level. "You guys are expendable. I've got to waste you."

15

A Taste of Fear

HOLDING HIS GUN ON THE DETECTIVES, DON Dellasandro quickly looked at his watch. "Okay, there's a little time before Big Barney's party at the Beverly Hilton." He reached into his other jacket pocket.

What now? thought Jupe.

Slowly Dellasandro pulled his hand out of his jacket, but he kept the hand closed. "We can network for a few minutes," he said. "Want to do some market research before you go belly up?"

"What do you mean?" asked Jupe, staring hard at Dellasandro's fist.

He opened his hand. He had more wrapped candies. "Try one," he said.

"It's poison, Jupe," Pete warned.

"Would I poison someone with taste buds like his? It's a shame I have to kill you, pal."

Jupe looked at Dellasandro, then at the gun, then at the candy, then at the clock on the wall. What good would it do to stall? The police weren't on their way. No one was coming to rescue them.

"I'd really value your input," Dellasandro said. "Unless you're in a big hurry to die. Tell me what you taste. Are my flavors on target?"

"Okay," Jupe said reluctantly. "I'll try it. But it's going to cost you."

"Everything has a price," Dellasandro said. "I used to think being a scientist was a noble profession. But without marketing skills it's just bottle pouring or germ breeding. Today if you can't tune into your channels, what good are you?"

"You can always get hooked up to cable," Bob said.

"Watch it!" Dellasandro said, suddenly wheeling toward Bob in anger. "I *hate* people who treat business like a joke! You're lucky your friend here is such a genius in the taste bud department, or you'd already be dead meat." He took two deep breaths to calm himself down and then added, "Dead meat is one of my best flavors, by the way."

Jupe held very still, as it dawned on him that Dellasandro was more than a little unhinged. Maybe he'd ingested too much Multisorbitane over the years.

"I'll try a piece of candy," Jupe said calmly. "But only on one condition. You've got to answer a question."

Dellasandro nodded and handed Jupe the candy. Jupe popped it into his mouth.

"Three tastes," Jupe said. "Lemon—real lemon essence, not imitation—meringue, and graham cracker crust. It's lemon meringue pie."

"Phenomenal," Dellasandro said.

"Now my turn," Jupe said. "This is Multisorbitane in these drums, the ones marked 'brominated pseudo-phosphates,' isn't it?"

"It is," Dellasandro said. "So what?"

"So what are you planning to use it for? I'm quite sure you know that it's an unacceptable food additive as far as the FDA is concerned."

"You want to ask another question? First you eat another candy. Pick one," Dellasandro said with a devilish grin. He held out his hand for Jupe to choose.

"Don't do it, Jupe. It's a trick," Pete said.

Jupe didn't really think the candy was poison, but he *did* think it might have Multisorbitane in it. Nonetheless, he had no choice. He wanted a confession from Dellasandro, and he wanted more time. He took a foil-wrapped candy from Dellasandro and tasted it.

"Cherry Jell-O with banana floaters and whipped cream," Jupe said, chomping down on the sample bonbon. "I've answered your question. Now answer mine. What are you going to do with these drums of Multisorbitane?"

Dellasandro took his time about answering. Finally he said, "Okay. I'll tell you—since we all know you won't be alive long enough to repeat it. Let me background a little. About a year ago, Big Barney Coop came to me. He wanted to collaborate on a new product, something no one had seen, tasted, or dreamed before—especially not Michael Argenti. He said he'd divide the profits with me and we were talking a dollar sign and then zeros off the page. But there were two conditions. One: the gravy had to be *in* the chicken. Two: it had to be sensationally delicious."

"Did Big Barney say to make it deadly?" Bob asked.

"*You* shut up!" Dellasandro shouted at Bob. More deep-breathing exercises. Then he was calm again. "Getting the gravy into the chicken turned out to be easy," Dellasandro continued. "Freeze-dried gravy injected as powder into the chicken fillets. When the chicken is fried at the restaurant, the gravy reconstitutes itself. The second puzzle was harder. How to irresistibilize the product. I tried every flavor, flavor savor, flavor enhancer, flavor duplicator I could think of for the gravy. They were good, but they weren't perfect."

"So you used Multisorbitane?" Jupe asked.

Dellasandro handed Jupe a third piece of candy. "Time was running out," he said, checking his watch. "I couldn't think of anything else to put in the gravy. My reputation and all those zeros after the dollar sign were at risk." Then Dellasandro noticed that Jupe wasn't eating the third candy. "What's the matter—are you *full*?"

"I'm saving it for dessert," Jupe said.

"Jupe, just remember he put a carcinogen into Drippin' Chicken," Bob warned.

"The cancer won't impact on people for ten or

twenty years," Dellasandro said. "That's a long time. No one will know. Big Barney won't know because I'm on the supply side of the gravy powder for his food processors. They'll send the prepared chicken to the restaurants, who interface with the customers directly. Everybody's happy, which is, after all, the highest goal of our civilization today."

Jupe looked at the clock on the wall again. It was almost eight, and he was almost out of ideas. His first analysis had been right: there was no point in stalling. Still, the impulse to buy more time was a hard one to ignore.

"I have one more question, if you'll allow me," Jupe said. "What made you come back here tonight?"

"I pay my security team well," Dellasandro replied. "The guard networked with me on my car phone as soon as you guys showed up." He looked at the last candy, which was still in Jupe's hand. "Eat your dessert, pal, because the bottom line is, your quality time is up."

Jupe unwrapped the candy. This one was different. It was hard and heavy in his hand. "Mr. Sweetness works for you, doesn't he?" said Jupe. "The guy in the army jacket."

"Mr. Sweetness?" Dellasandro laughed. "Highly original. Yeah, Vinnie's my next-door neighbor. Got a pink slip from the marines, I understand. They seemed to think he was too vicious to be a real team player. The moment Juliet mentioned at Big Barney's party that you were detectives, I strategized that Vinnie could help me scare you guys off. I told him to do whatever he had to do. First he tapped your phone."

"So that's how he knew we ordered Chinese food," Jupe realized.

"Yeah, he took the ball and ran with it. I was very impressed with his creativity. But somehow you kept getting away from him." Dellasandro waved his gun toward Jupe's mouth. "Eat the candy," he said.

"Don't do it, Jupe," Pete warned.

Jupe slowly put the candy into his mouth. After a moment, he said, "Caramel."

"Just wait," said Don Dellasandro, smiling.

Jupe chewed some more and then said, "Oh, very clever. It's caramel apple. Now I can taste the apple."

"Mr. Sweetness—that's what I'll call that flavor," Dellasandro said. "I'll flash on you every time some-one says it."

"You're a brilliant scientist, a clever marketing man, but a terrible killer," said Jupe.

"In this new age we can't always do what we like, but we have to do what's important," Dellasandro replied. "In my mind I can image myself wasting you three."

"Not with the safety catch locked on your gun," said Jupe.

"It is?" Dellasandro said, looking down.

Pete didn't wait. He moved instinctively into a flying *yoko-tobi-geri* side kick, connecting with Dellasandro's hand. The gun flew into the air and clattered on the ground.

Then Pete and Bob both charged Dellasandro, but the older man was strong and quick. He seemed to know some karate moves too. He gave Bob a quick kick in the knee, which sent Bob down. Then Dellasandro spun and arced a ridge hand at Pete. Pete blocked the blow and gave Dellasandro a *gyaku-tsuki* reverse punch to the ribs. The scientist winced and staggered backward. Pete leaped into the air, twisting and lifting his feet high.

"*Aiiiya*," Pete screamed, knocking Dellasandro down.

But Dellasandro rolled and stood up. He looked around. Then he saw the gun on the floor a second before Jupe did. He rushed to grab it. "I'm terminating this meeting!" he shouted.

16

Big Barney Wings It

DELLASANDRO DOVE FOR THE REVOLVER. JUPE grabbed frantically for it at the same time, but he was just a moment too late. Dellasandro actually laughed when he picked up the gun. Then he stood up to face the Three Investigators.

It wasn't until then that Dellasandro realized he had paid too much attention to the gun—and too little attention to the three guys he was fighting. Because just then a heavy drum marked BROMINATED PSEUDO-PHOSPHATES, but actually filled with Multisorbitane, came flying through the air.

Pete and Bob had lifted it together and heaved it at Dellasandro. The drum hit him like a wrecking ball, knocking him down and out. It burst open when it struck the floor, dumping hundreds of pounds of Multisorbitane over everything, even on the chemist who had invented it.

"Talk about getting a taste of your own medicine," Bob said with a whistle.

Pete and Jupe quickly tied up Dellasandro with extension cords. Shortly Dellasandro began to regain consciousness.

"What happened?" Dellasandro asked groggily.

"You didn't miss much," Jupe replied. "You gave us a full confession and then there was a fight and you lost. Now you're tied up."

"There's no time to call the police," Bob said. "We'll have to catch them later tonight."

"Police?" Dellasandro echoed.

"Yes," Jupe said. "We're pressing charges for your small indiscretion in hiring someone to follow us, trying to market an illegal food additive, and threatening to kill us. I think at least one of those charges will stick. But first we've got to get to the Beverly Hilton Hotel. Come on, you guys."

It was a half-hour drive, cut shorter by the fact that Pete drove. They pulled up in front of the hotel and ran through the lobby. The press party, a sign said, was about to begin in the Empire Ballroom.

The Investigators ran past the ballroom entrances and headed right for the kitchen. There they found Big Barney in a yellow jogging suit covered with orange and red feathers. Juliet and Pandro Mishkin were standing by him. And almost every inch of kitchen counter space was covered with steaming trays of Drippin' Chicken.

"Hey, guy," Big Barney said as soon as he saw Jupe. He wrapped his arm around Jupe's shoulder. "Tell me the truth, even though I may never speak to you again and will probably try to ruin your life if I don't like the answer—is this outfit too conservative?"

"Big Barney, forget about your outfit. You can't go out there," Jupe said. "Drippin' Chicken is deadly. It's filled with a dangerous carcinogen. You've got to cancel this party and withdraw the product—or millions of people will die."

Big Barney stared at Jupe and the noisy, clattering kitchen fell silent. Then suddenly Big Barney burst into laughter. "Hahahaha! You almost had me. I'm telling you I've got to have this guy for my son."

"Look! Mishkin's getting away!" Bob shouted.

Everyone did look. And what they saw was Pandro Mishkin trying to sprint out of the kitchen.

Pete and Bob and Jupe immediately grabbed the first thing they could get their hands on. It was a long baker's tray piled high with Drippin' Chicken. They heaved it at the fleeing man, hitting him in the back. Drippin' Chicken splattered everywhere. Then Pete made a diving leap, grabbed Pandro Mishkin at the shoulders, and brought him down in a smear of gravy, like a wide receiver in the mud.

"Complete and utter insubordination!" Mishkin yelled, struggling with Pete. "You could be court-martialed for this."

"It's you who will be going to court, Mr. Mishkin," Jupe said, "for poisoning the Drippin' Chicken."

"Torture me if you want but all you'll get is my name, rank, and serial number. I won't talk," Mishkin said proudly.

"You don't really have to," Jupe said. "Don Della-sandro told us just about everything we need to know—including how you paid him to poison Big Barney's chicken."

"The lying traitor!" cried Mishkin. "*He* paid *me*!"

Jupe couldn't help smiling. "You're right," he said. "My mistake."

"What are you talking about, Mishkin?" Big Barney asked, his eyes wide with disbelief. "Give me your report!"

"General," Pandro answered, "your Drippin' Chicken is filled with an additive the FDA outlawed a few years ago. How do you like them apples?"

"You betrayed me?" Big Barney boomed.

"You didn't pay me a million dollars. And Don Dellasandro did," Mishkin replied.

"And all you had to do was falsify the ingredients of Drippin' Chicken," said Jupe.

"A million bucks buys a lot of loyalty from this soldier," Mishkin said. "I should have gone merce-nary a long time ago."

Big Barney rushed over to Mishkin and tore the chicken medals off his jacket. "I'd like to wring your neck!" Big Barney shouted.

Jupe stepped between them and asked one more question. "*You* were the one chasing Juliet Coop the night of her accident, weren't you?"

"Correct," Mishkin said.

"Why, Mr. Mishkin?" asked Juliet. She held her father's arm tightly, as if needing the support.

"The report was on my desk, along with a list of ingredients for Drippin' Chicken. You were working late—without prior authorization! You saw the papers and started yelling the minute I walked in the door. The darn thing was stamped 'Top Secret'! You ought to be thrown in the stockade for reading classified materials!"

"So Juliet grabbed the report and you chased her," Jupe said.

"Yes," Mishkin said. "But I wasn't trying to hurt her." He looked directly at Juliet. "When your car went off the road in the rain, it was an accident. On my honor."

"Why didn't you do something to help her?" said Big Barney.

"I did. I stopped . . . I wanted to help her. But I had to protect my identity. So I called the police and made a complete report about the accident—anonymously, of course."

"Dad," Juliet said a little breathlessly, "I'm remembering it now. The crash—it was horrible!" She was almost crying. Big Barney put his arm around his daughter.

"For a while we thought Michael Argenti was behind this whole scheme," Jupe said to Big Barney. "We followed him to one of your chicken farms and heard him talking about buying you out and changing the feed."

"That little cockerel doesn't know the difference between chicken feed and chicken salad. He changes his feed all the time. It must make his birds want to commit suicide," said Big Barney. "But he doesn't have enough money to buy me out, even in his dreams."

"You even thought Dad was a suspect, admit it, Jupe," said Juliet.

"Well," Jupe said uncomfortably, "I couldn't figure out why you were spitting out the Drippin' Chicken after every take at the recording studio."

"Everybody does that in food commercials," Big Barney explained. "If you swallow the food every time, after thirty takes you're full to the beak. Then you can't look so happy about having to take another bite during take number thirty-one."

Juliet turned to her father. "Dad, you've got a hundred hungry press people out there," she said. "What are you going to do now?"

Big Barney fluffed his feathers for a moment, preening in thought. Then with a smile he said, "You just watch me."

He rushed out into the ballroom and took his usual place—in the spotlight and behind a microphone.

"Good evening, ladies and germs. Hahahaha!" he began. "Now, I suppose you're wondering why I called you all here tonight. I know that most of you think that Big Barney's only out for a quick buck and a fast headline. So I guess you know me pretty well."

The audience joined in with Barney's laughing this time.

"Folks, I'm not here tonight to plug my delicious

and famous fried chicken. And to prove it, in a few minutes we're all going to be sending out for"—Big Barney choked a little on the next word—"pizza! That's right. Pizza! And I'm sure you're almost as surprised as I am about that." Big Barney wiped his brow with a feathered arm. "But folks, I'm proud to announce something brand new," he continued. "Tonight I am announcing the first ever Big Barney City Slicker Award, an award I plan to present every year to people who help to make this city a better place to live in. Now, because I'm too modest to give this award to myself, I'd like to anounce tonight's winners. And here they are and I love them like my own kids: Junior Jones, Pete Cranberry, and Bob Andersonville—better known to all of us as The Three Instigators. I'm honoring them in particular tonight for all the things they do *behind* the scenes—things you may not know about but that we're all grateful for. So let's give them a round of applause, folks, and tell them how we feel."

As the audience applauded, Jupe, Pete, and Bob walked up into the spotlight, although Big Barney was taking up most of it.

Barney shook their hands and gave them lots of freebie coupons while waving and smiling at the TV cameras.

"Hey, guys, can't thank you enough," Big Barney said. "And I'm going to be floating on this publicity for months."

"Anytime," Jupe said with a sigh.

"Yeah, glad we could maximize you," said Bob.

"For sure," said Pete.

"Don't look so hoof and mouth, guys," said Big Barney. "Once your names hit the media with this award, you'll be on the map. And always remember who put you there. Yours ever so truly. Hahahaha!"